I Took Panama

RODOLFO M. LEITÓN

LCCN: 2012916938
ISBN-13: 978-1469915265
ISBN-10: 146991526X

www.itookpanama.com

www.facebook.com/itookpanama

DEDICATION

For Elke, the love of my life, who encouraged me to write this book.

For Emiliano and Amadeo, who motivate me every day to be a better person.

ACKNOWLEDGMENTS

This book was written over the course of many nights, weekends, and some vacation time. The support and understanding of my wife and children were vital and without their constant encouragement, this novel probably wouldn't exist. It was Elke, who, after listening to me comment several times that someone ought to write a novel about Bunau-Varilla, suggested that I do it myself.

My mother, Ana Victoria, who is an extraordinary painter and oral storyteller, continually encouraged me to complete this project. My father, Rodolfo, taught me by example, the value of perseverance and hard work, which were invaluable in the face of seemingly never-ending research and the synthesis of so much information.

Dailey Wallace, curator of the Theodore Roosevelt Collection at Harvard University; John Armstrong at Wright State University in Dayton, Ohio; and Jéremy Barande, from the Office of Communications at the *École Polytechnique* in France, allowed me access to resources necessary to the materialization of this book.

Frank Arre, from the Unites States Naval History and Heritage Command, kindly contributed photos surrounding the sinking of the U.S.S. Maine to use as illustrations.

In Panama, I had the support of Irina de Ardila, who brought me into contact with Mr. Ricardo López Arias in Barcelona, who shared with me various hard to obtain photos of Bunau-Varilla during his stay in Panama. Also, Rolando Cochez Lara, Administrator at the Roberto F. Chiari Library in Panama, kindly and patiently helped me when I asked on several occasions for his help in acquiring more information.

Magali Lacouse of the National Archives in Paris allowed me access to documents which were extremely important to my investigation, most notably, Bunau-Varilla's birth certificate. Rebecca Garnier, manager of the Paris restaurant, *Le Procope,* was kind enough to send me information about the types of food that have been served in her establishment over the centuries.

Gerald Gómez of the Procter & Gamble Company generously devoted time from his busy schedule to help me locate a photo of Harley Thomas Procter in the corporate archives. Jim Sluzewski and Scott Byers of Macy´s Inc., kindly provided historical images to help illustrate the book.

Gabriel Loizillon, the French writer who produced one of the most revealing books about the Bunau-Varilla brothers and the origins of their fortune, kindly corresponded with me on several occasions. Valeria Rocco, descendent of Philippe Bunau-Varilla, patiently listened to some of my ideas regarding this book, made suggestions, and recommended sources of information which were incredibly useful to my investigation.

Daniel Quesada thoroughly reviewed the manuscript and suggested ways in which to greatly improve the content. Mía Gallegos Domínguez helped to polish my modest draft; her assistance significantly improved this novel. Finally, Nikki Settelmeyer did a wonderful job translating my story into English while maintaining the "personality" of the Spanish.

PROLOGUE

On May 15, 1879, the Geographic Society of Paris organized the Universal Congress, an international event to determine the best route for the construction of an interoceanic canal in Central America.

Previously, Ferdinand de Lesseps, famed engineer of the Suez Canal and member of the Geographic Society, had chaired a committee that negotiated a treaty which gave France exclusive rights to construct a canal in the Colombian province of Panama. Therefore, when the Universal Congress convened, France had a definite interest in the Panamanian route being selected.

During the event, more than ten possible canal routes were evaluated, but Nicaragua and Panama were selected the best options.

In spite of technically superior information presented by the Americans to promote the Nicaraguan route, and of the mediocre defense presented by de Lesseps' collaborators, the French majority prevailed in the final vote and the Panamanian route won by 74 votes in favor and eight against.

Ferdinand de Lesseps' proposal to construct a canal at sea level and without any locks was approved in spite of the opposing votes of French engineers Godin de Lépinay, who had proposed a canal with locks and an artificial lake to reduce the amount of excavation, and Alexander Gustave Eiffel.

"I took Panama because Bunau-Varilla brought it to me on a silver platter."

President Theodore Roosevelt, to William Morton Fullerton

during a visit to Oyster Bay

1

Paris, October 1881

Philippe pushed his way through the other students—all of them older and most of them much taller. Attending a speech given by "Le Grand Français" was an opportunity he couldn't miss; he had waited years to meet him and didn't know if he'd ever again get the chance.

The doors would be closing any moment and he hadn't gotten in yet, so he quickened his pace as much as possible in his constricting blue uniform, worn by all the students at the prestigious Polytechnic School. To have been accepted by the military institution on a scholarship two years earlier, at nineteen years old, was a great source of pride for Philippe. Statesmen, philosophers, scientists, and other exemplary countrymen had graduated from the institution and it was there, at the Polytechnic School, where he too should be educated.

On this visit, Ferdinand de Lesseps would reveal to the teachers and student body the findings of his recent expedition to Panama, which had been chosen by several countries as the location for construction of the interoceanic canal during the Universal Congress in Paris which took place two years earlier.

Being so near de Lesseps filled Philippe with emotion difficult to describe. He could still remember a time when he was a child and an engineer who had worked with de Lesseps in Egypt on the construction of the Suez Canal had come to his home. During the visit, Philippe had been so excited by the engineer's story, he announced to his mother that one day he too would build canals

1

around the world. "You're too young for Suez, but you can still build Panama," his mother had said, and the boy never forgot those words.

Making his way through the crowd, Philippe held on tight to the card that identified him as a special guest of General Pourrat, his sponsor at the "X," as the Polytechnic School was more popularly known. To be left out of the lecture and miss the opportunity to see and hear "Le Grand Français" was unthinkable. Just then, barely two meters from the entrance, a guard announced that the auditorium was full and that no one else would be permitted inside. People begged and pleaded, and someone tried to force their way through the closing doors.

What he lacked in height and build, he made up for with his strong character and overpowering gaze. "I am a guest of General Pourrat, let me in!" Philippe said, showing his invite to the guard. Once inside, he managed to find an empty seat at the front of the auditorium, just meters from where de Lesseps would be speaking.

If "Le Grand Français" had been able to build the Suez Canal, he would, without a doubt, be successful in the Caribbean, from where he had just returned. Although everyone had read the reports about his expedition, there was great fascination in getting to listen to the story, directly from de Lesseps' own mouth.

Next to the podium was a strange wooden and metal apparatus pointed toward a piece of white fabric at the front of the auditorium. "A magic lantern! Surely they are going to show us pictures of the Colombian expedition. Excellent!" Philippe thought to himself.

Amid the applause, Philippe heard the doors close and as he turned to his right, he could see Ferdinand de Lesseps heading toward the podium. He wore his thick white hair combed to the left. In spite of his 75 years, his strong and energetic stride was that of a man thirty years younger. His black double-breasted suit and matching tie beneath the collar of his bulging white shirt, gave an air of undeniable elegance.

But the famous mustache with waxed tips pointing upward caught Philippe's attention more than anything else. As he watched de Lesseps smoothly make his way to the front of the auditorium, Philippe tried to twist the tips of his own modest mustache in the same fashion.

Philippe Bunau-Varilla's graduation photo from the Polytechnic School
Courtesy of the Polytechnic School; © Ecole Polytechnique.

Ferdinand de Lesseps approached the podium and the auditorium fell silent, anxiously awaiting his lecture. Meanwhile, "Le Grand Français" was clearly satisfied by his observation of the students and professors. Even though he was looking out over the entire auditorium, Philippe swore that he was the intended recipient of his idol's famous smile.

After welcoming all those in attendance and extending his thanks for having been invited, de Lesseps got right to the point: "For centuries, the civilized nations of the world have wanted to build an interoceanic canal in Central America. The first to suggest building it in the Colombian province of Panama was the Spanish explorer, Álvaro de Cerón in 1517.

"Hundreds of years later, Alexander von Humboldt proposed nine possible routes for the interoceanic canal, and later chose Panama as the best place for construction. And two years ago, the Universal Congress took place here in Paris, and delegates from 36 countries also determined that the Panamanian route is indeed the best.

"A centuries-old Grand Idea that we are now able to put into action. French scientific advances and modern engineering allow us to embark on projects that, in decades past, would have been impossible even to imagine. The proof is in Egypt…"

At this moment, de Lesseps' assistant turned on the magic lantern and, to the audience's surprise, an image of the Suez Canal was projected behind the podium. The auditorium erupted with delight. Someone from the back shouted, "Long live 'Le Grand Français'! Long live the Suez Canal!" and many others joined in.

De Lesseps smiled and gestured for the crowd to be quiet, "The Suez Canal, which was built in large part by students from this very school, has linked Asia and Europe, facilitating commerce and benefitting millions of people. And now, just as I did 21 years ago, I've come to invite the best engineers in the world to join me in this new and exciting venture: the interoceanic canal in the Colombian province of Panama!"

The magic lantern now projected a map of Panama, with the proposed route clearly marked. The auditorium was ecstatic. Someone screamed, "We're going to Panama! We'll build the canal!" And he was seconded by a professor who sang out the Polytechnic School's motto, "For country, science, and honor!"

When it quieted down, de Lesseps continued in a more serious tone, "Recently I visited Panama; I was accompanied by our international technical committee and our objective was to inspect the route in which the canal will be built, as required by the treaty with the Colombian government."

The auditorium had fallen completely silent.

"We arrived on December 30th, on the steamship *Lafayette*. On the Bahía de Limón, we were received with a warm welcome from the Panamanian people, who were happy that the canal was finally going to be built." Then he added, with a mischievous smile, "In fact, the local government representative, Mr. Céspedes, jokingly asked why it had taken the French so long to decide to build the canal there. Let us bring peace and prosperity to the people who have welcomed us with open arms!

"Furthermore, as my son Charles said, that part of Colombia is the most beautiful place in the world. And the climate, the climate is perfect: it's the land of eternal spring." Someone seated behind Philippe murmured, "Obviously, if he visited the Caribbean at the beginning of summer, I imagine the weather would have been fantastic!"

Without waiting for the initial applause to end, de Lesseps continued, "But, getting back to the purpose of our visit, I have to tell you that after several weeks of personally inspecting the proposed route of construction for the canal, we came to several very important conclusions."

De Lesseps made himself comfortable at the podium, stroking his upward pointing mustache with his right index finger and thumb, and watched with satisfaction as the entire auditorium leaned forward to better hear him, "The first is that, compared to the construction of the Suez Canal, excavating the Panama Canal will be much easier."

Various expressions of surprise could be heard throughout the crowd.

"To start, the distance between the oceans is very short; in fact, it's similar to the distance between Paris and *Fontainbleau*. According to Abel Couvrex, Jr., we will have to utilize the same excavation techniques that were used in Egypt because the terrain is very similar. So, the experience we gained in Suez will greatly benefit us in Panama."

De Lesseps continued, "We've also concluded that the

construction will take only eight years, and not twelve, as we had initially thought. This reduction in time will significantly reduce our construction costs. The funds we had estimated at first will no longer be necessary: we only need half! We've already managed to save a great deal and we haven't even begun!"

Ferdinand de Lesseps had the audience just where he wanted them. "So friends, the construction of the Panama Canal will be more economical and less time-consuming than we originally thought. Those who can, buy stocks when they go on sale! I believe that the Panama Canal Company will be much more profitable than that of the Suez Canal." Everyone recalled that the value of the Suez Canal Company's shares had quadrupled since they were issued. If "Le Grand Français" stressed that Panama would also be a good investment, surely it was true.

"But beyond the financial aspect, I believe that we French have been blessed with the responsibility of accomplishing great works which will benefit humanity. The achievement of this Grand Idea, will demonstrate to the world that, in spite of recent difficulties, France will continue to be France!" The audience fell silent, remembering the recent defeat against Germany.

"We have already gotten approval from the Colombian government to begin construction as soon as possible. And there is no time to lose!" de Lesseps exclaimed to the delight of his audience. "It pleases me to tell you that in January of next year, Gastón Blanchet, engineer and general director of our operations, will depart for Panama. He will work with our friends at Couvreux, Hersent & Company, and hopefully, also with many of you."

He paused again to curl his mustache, and then continued, "Because the Universal Congress chose Panama, the route favored by the French, over the Nicaraguan route, which was selected by the Americans, it is vital that we get the support of the United States. Some might say the Monroe Doctrine requires it. So from Panama, we departed to New York to invite Andrew Carnegie, John Bigelow, J.P. Morgan, and other illustrious Americans to participate as shareholders in the Canal Company. In addition, we offered to put up Company offices in New York. Ours will be a truly international effort," he concluded, solemnly.

"Therefore, my friends," he said, growing emotional, affecting the entire auditorium as he spoke slowly and clearly, "we know what we have to do, we know how to do it, and we have the resources necessary to do it. The canal will be built! The canal will be built! Join in this great venture and support France in living the motto of this great institution! For country, science, and honor!" Now the magic lantern showed an illustration of the earth wrapped in the French flag.

The entire auditorium stood up to applaud for several minutes while Ferdinand de Lesseps, with a white handkerchief, wiped away tears of joy brought on by his own speech, before leaving the podium to embrace General Pourrat.

Ferdinand de Lesseps
Public domain image.

2

That weekend, Philippe left the Polytechnic School Annex to visit his grandmother and mother, Caroline Pamela, as he did every weekend. When he arrived, he realized his older brother, Maurice, was also home. Philippe loved and admired Maurice, who had recently begun working at the *Crédit Lyonnais* Bank. With firm resolution, his brother maintained the family while Philippe devoted himself entirely to his studies.

The four of them sat in the modest Bunau kitchen, and after beginning to eat a meal of rack of lamb and scalloped potatoes, Philippe said enthusiastically, "Mother, I know what I'm going to do after graduation—I'm going to Panama to build a canal with Ferdinand de Lesseps!"

Upon hearing these words, his mother choked and then began coughing. Maurice had to get up immediately to help her compose herself. As she drank from her glass of water, his grandmother, with a worried look in her eye, asked, "You've seen him?"

"Yes, Grandma, Mr. de Lesseps is an extraordinary man. What they say about him in the papers doesn't do him justice. There is so much to his personality... magnetic like you can't imagine. He came to the Polytechnic School to invite the students to join him on the canal project."

The women looked at each other without saying a word. Maurice spoke up, "But students have to work five years for the state before joining a private enterprise. How can he recruit students from the Polytechnic School?"

Still smiling, Philippe responded, "Well, since the Panama Canal is considered a project of national interest, exceptions are being made for students. After I graduate and serve a bit of time in the Civil Service, I can request special permission to be allowed to work in Panama. Mr. Schwoebele offered to help me."

Philippe's mother said only, "What's he like? Have you spoken to him? Have you spent time with him?"

Philippe responded with a smile, "Of course, mother, I see Mr. Schwoebele every day."

Mamie, his grandmother intervened, "She's talking about Mr. de Lesseps, Philippe."

"No mother, I wasn't able to introduce myself. Everyone wanted to talk to him and it was impossible for me to get any closer. But when I work on the construction of the canal, surely I'll have the opportunity to meet and speak to him. Imagine, Maurice, working with 'Le Grand Français' and building a new canal!" While Philippe talked with Maurice, who was also excited about de Lesseps' speech, both women ate in silence, never even looking up from their plates.

3

Construction of the Panama Canal, Colombia, March 1885

It was seven in the morning and in spite of the torrential rain, Philippe had already been inspecting the excavation site for two hours. Gustave, his assistant, held an umbrella that covered them both as they walked uphill on a path that was more like a stream. Today, like the last three days, the downpour had made advancing the excavation all but impossible.

With his boots covered in mud and his fine clothing soaking wet, Philippe held his derby hat so the wind wouldn't carry it away. He'd never been in the habit of wearing Hawkes styled English hats or clothing like the other engineers wore, which seemed unsuitable for the momentous job they were working on.

Philippe had arrived in Panama six months earlier on the same ship as his new boss, Dingler, the general director, who was returning from France with his wife after a short vacation. Dingler's son, daughter, and son-in-law were buried in the Panamanian soil after succumbing to tropical sicknesses a year before.

The journey lasted weeks, during which Philippe had dedicated himself to impressing Jules Dingler and demonstrating how much he had studied for the job to be done, particularly on the Culebra Cut: the section where the majority of the excavation would take place. The young engineer succeeded in making his mark on the general director.

From the top of the mountain, and while Gustave did what he

could to protect his superior from the rain, Philippe observed thousands of workers using picks and shovels, trying to widen the small crack that was the beginning of the Culebra Cut. Alongside the workers, huge machines blew smoke while depositing mud and rocks in small wagons responsible for collecting and removing the materials. From there, Culebra was a green bulge crossed by a band of brown, swarming with men and machines.

It was a spectacular view that Philippe enjoyed every day. He was constructing a canal for France and for the world, and the dream he'd had since he was only ten years old was coming true. The view also reminded him of the engineer who had visited his childhood home after returning from working in Suez.

But Panama wasn't the land of "eternal spring" as de Lesseps had promised. And the terrain they were excavating couldn't be worked in "the same way as in Europe," like Abel Couvreux had said. The strange mixture of clay, sandstone, and silt that made up the Culebra Cut turned out to be unstable, and with the torrential rain it collapsed almost daily, refilling what had been excavated, at times submerging entire brigades of workers in the landslide.

The contractors, responsible for practically the entire excavation, did their best to try to fulfill their obligations in the most economic and profitable way, with little regard for actual progress of the job. In the last year, the excavation on Culebra averaged only one meter in depth. Still, many of them threatened to pull out if the Canal Company didn't improve contractual conditions, a request that was generally accepted.

There had also been problems with labor. The black French-speaking workers fought the black Spanish-speakers with machetes. Some blacks who had been slaves until only recently refused to follow the orders of team leaders, claiming they were "free men." And several of the Chinese didn't want to work on the excavation at all anymore, and turned instead to commerce.

If the workers weren't working or drunk, they were probably sick. Although many illnesses afflicted people on the isthmus, there were two which took the majority of lives: the swampy emanations from the excavation caused malaria, so the more they excavated, the more people fell ill. The predominant filth in Cólon was the cause of yellow fever. Marcus Schouwe, the contractor in charge of importing labor, couldn't fill positions with the same speed that illnesses were creating new vacancies.

The diseases were so lethal than many people perished even during short visits to Panama. Philippe remembered cases such as the *Dolphin*, a ship carrying wood from New Orleans that had stopped in Colón to replenish necessities, and weeks later, was still tied to the dock: the entire crew had died and there was no one left to captain the orphan ship to other ports.

But Philippe wasn't afraid of disease. In fact, he visited the hospitals on a daily basis. There, he encouraged the many workers who were dying, he greeted the patients, shook their hands, and joked with those who could still do so. Sometimes, his visits were interrupted when he had to make room for coffins placed beside the beds of those he was visiting.

He wasn't afraid of contracting diseases because malaria attacked people with weak morals; he was protected by his lack of fear. Furthermore, a local healer had recommended a mixture of quinine and brandy that had kept several American engineers healthy during construction of the railroad. Surely this would protect Philippe.

In spite of all the bad things that were taking place in Panama, including the numerous deaths of his colleagues, disorder and bureaucracy within the company, as well as the dishonest and corrupt contractors, Philippe was happy to be there. He was living the dream he'd had since he was a child: to join two oceans just like "Le Grand Français" had done in Suez.

In fact, before coming to Panama, he'd already known of all the risks to which he would be exposed. The Parisian newspapers, in spite of the efforts of the Canal Company to hide such occurrences, had been reporting for some time the deaths of many known Frenchmen as a result of diseases. When, before departure, Mr. Schwoebele asked why he'd want to expose himself to so much danger by going to Panama, Philippe had responded without hesitation, "For the same reason a soldier goes to battle, Mr. Schwoebele."

Philippe and a group of engineers in Panama. He is second from the left, in the derby hat. Jules Dingler is seated in the center, wearing white pants and resting his hands on an umbrella.
Photo courtesy of Ricardo López Arias.

4

March 16, 1885

Philippe had just boarded the aging train to Colón and was walking toward the car reserved for Canal Company employees. Observing the seats, it was hard to believe that during the gold rush, thousands of adventurers had taken this very train as a shortcut to California. The American passengers no longer needed to come to Panama; for the past two years, it had been possible to travel from New York to San Francisco in only four days by way of one of the new intercontinental trains.

Now the cars on this train were almost always empty: Philippe counted seven passengers that day, including a railroad employee, Dr. Manuel Amador, who he greeted cordially. The doctor was almost twice Philippe's age, but between the two of them there was a mutual respect that had flourished during the French engineer's visits to the hospitals.

This train, whose original owners were from New York, was now property of the Canal Company. Ferdinand de Lesseps had recently bought it for twice its market value so he wouldn't have to depend on the Americans, and in doing so, simplified the process of constructing the canal. "A terrible investment, but it had to be done…" thought Philippe, now in his seat.

Even though the train's shares had switched hands, the United States still maintained their commitment, acquired four decades earlier, to guarantee Colombian sovereignty over Panama and ensure free passage by railroad. American forces remained on both coasts. Another familiar passenger, seated near Amador, was Captain Mahan of the gunboat, *Wachusett*, who was probably returning from a meeting with his colleagues stationed on the Pacific Coast.

That afternoon, Philippe was going to meet with H.B. Slaven, one of the many opportunists who had come to the isthmus seeking treasure and who had effortlessly found it. Educated in pharmacy, Slaven knew nothing about excavations, but when he heard about the lucrative contracts being signed in Panama, he made several offers for different sections of the canal and, to his surprise, some were accepted. Slaven secured funding in New York, purchased excavators, contracted operators in Philadelphia and so began a successful business. When Philippe saw the payments to be made to the pharmacist, he thought enviously, "How fortunate…"

Upon arrival at the station, Philippe stepped onto the platform and began walking toward Slaven's offices. He hated to visit Colón because of the filth. Covering his nose with a handkerchief, perfumed to shield him from the smell of feces and garbage typical of the city, he turned to avoid a pile of empty wine bottles in the middle of the sidewalk.

As he was walking, he noticed some engineers from the company coming out of La Constancia, the most popular brothel among French expatriates, as four sweaty, half-naked prostitutes waved their goodbyes from the balcony. Seeing Philippe, who continued walking with his head held high and not turning to look at them, they greeted him "Good day, Sir," and ashamed, quickened their pace.

Passing the entrance to a bar, he was almost hit by a man coming out to throw his trash in the street. Scraps of food, bottles and a bloodstained shirt fell at Philippe's feet. On the walk in front of him, the rotting corpse of a horse was being devoured by vultures that appeared oblivious of the people passing by. On the verge of vomiting from disgust at the surrounding scene, Philippe heard shots behind him.

The Colombian Army had gone to Cartagena to pacify a rebellion, leaving the city of Colón without protection, so a local group of rebels had taken the opportunity to seize the city. "Death to Núñez! Long live the Liberal Party!" they shouted as they marched in the street. Their leader, a small mulatto lawyer named Pedro Prestán, steered them with authority as more and more citizens joined in.

Philippe ran to the company offices where, amid a group of frightened French bureaucrats, he found Dr. Amador.

"Mr. Bunau-Varilla, they are threatening to burn the city to the ground! The rebellion began hours ago... General Vila is coming to restore order, he left on the last train from Panama City!"

Philippe knew that Panama was politically unstable, but since arriving the year before, he hadn't been faced with a conflict of this magnitude. "Doctor, what do the rebels want?" he asked.

"The same as always, we want to be independent from Colombia. For more than fifty years we've been hearing promises of equal treatment from Bogotá, but we're still a third class territory," the doctor explained. "Mr. Bunau-Varilla, I'm going to the hospital to make sure the patients won't be affected by the revolt," he said while crossing the threshold to leave.

After Amador had gone, Philippe looked for a pen to write a message to Dingler asking for instructions. "Protect the buildings and machinery. Continue operations without interruption," was the response received hours later from Panama City. So, in the coming weeks, Philippe and his colleague, Maurice Hutin, dedicated themselves, as per Dingler's orders, to protecting the assets of the Canal Company and of the railroad. It was essential that they continued operating.

During this time, the rebellion spread to Panama City where yet another rebel, Aizpuru, proposed to declare Panama independent from Colombia if the United States would recognize him as leader of the new government. For several weeks, separatists and federalists fought in the streets of both cities and in the jungle, leaving dozens dead. Prestán went so far as to take American soldiers hostage to demand they hand over the weapons they'd been holding from him. But in spite of everything that happened, the American soldiers didn't do anything to detain the rebellion because they hadn't received orders from Washington.

It wasn't until the rebels had attacked and burned almost all the buildings in the city of Colón, that at the request of President Rafael Núñez, the United States authorized various ships under the command of Admiral James Jouett to restore order in Panama. Soon, Colombian troops arrived under the direction of General Reyes and the revolt was put to an end. Once more, Colombia had maintained unity thanks to American intervention.

5

August 1885

Everyone said that Jules Dingler had gone crazy after the death of his wife, the last member of his family lost to malaria. The day of the funeral, January 1, he had gone to work at his office, like any other day. After the burial, he'd taken his horse, his wife's horse, and his children's horses to a hill near his house where he shot them. From then on, every day was a nightmare for the director and his team.

From morning to night, Dingler screamed orders, taking only small breaks during which he'd rock in his chair with his head in his hands to try to relieve the agony that gnawed at his brain. On one occasion, several engineers had to restrain Dingler to keep him from throwing an accountant from his plaza-facing office balcony for having agreed to pay for a mysterious shipment of ink barrels sent from the office in New York.

By August, he couldn't take any more. He sent a telegram to Paris affirming his resignation, packed all his possessions, and ordered that his carriage be prepared to embark. Before departing, he stopped at the cemetery to say goodbye to his family. He wept bitterly for an hour but never lost his composure, and when he was ready, he kissed the headstones and got back into the carriage.

Passing through Colón, he noticed a number of people gathered at the railroad tracks. Over the rails, a wooden structure had been built, and from it, a thin rope was hanging and being greased by the port captain, an American by the name of Harris who had been a vigilante in the American West where he often acted as judge and executioner.

A brown-skinned man, dressed in a suit and tie over a white shirt, was helped onto a train car platform situated below the knot. Removing his derby hat and revealing his curly hair, he kept repeating that he was innocent, that he hadn't tried to burn the city, and then he blew a kiss to a woman who was crying as she covered the eyes of a boy who didn't understand what was happening. A soldier in tattered clothing put the rope on the man's neck, allowed Pedro Prestán to replace his derby hat, and Captain Harris immediately gave the order to move the platform on which the condemned man stood.

The hanging of Pedro Prestán.
Photo courtesy of the Panama Canal Authority.

At the port, Maurice Hutin and Philippe were waiting for Dingler. The two senior engineers at the Canal Company saw Dingler as a model of honesty, hard work, and perseverance in the face of adversity. Both were dismayed by the abandonment of their boss. Hutin, a tall and well-built man with the heart of a child, had been chosen as the new general director. "Mr. Dingler, it has been an honor to work with you," Maurice said, trying unsuccessfully to hold back his tears, which caused great discomfort to both Dingler and

Philippe.

"Don't follow my example; don't abandon Panama," said the defeated engineer before hugging the two men and boarding the *Lafayette*.

Two weeks after having assumed direction of the company, Maurice contracted yellow fever. Crying inconsolably in times of lucidity, he begged for his life so he could return to his family. In the fourth week, he began to show signs of improvement and as soon as he could, he packed his things and told his colleague he would be returning to France. "Forgive me for leaving, Philippe, but I can't risk my life for an enterprise that might not make it to the end of the year. The company is almost bankrupt, can't you see? We have barely progressed and they say the money is almost gone…"

Philippe interrupted, "Have you forgotten our agreement? Have you forgotten the Polytechnic School motto? The canal will be completed; 'Le Grand Français' will know how to solve all of these problems. We have to finish the canal in any way we can. Don't be a coward!"

"Don't you realize what is happening? We haven't made any progress and they say there is no money for the project, the Americans want to sabotage our work to take over the canal and every day there are more deaths. Like I said, I'm sorry but I'm going. And no, no I haven't forgotten the motto, but I can help to complete the canal from Paris." And with that, Maurice Hutin left Panama.

With no other candidates willing to take on the position at the moment, the Canal Company had to elect the engineer of highest rank as director, and so the position was given to Philippe Bunau-Varilla. At only twenty-six years old, he was put in charge of France's most important project of the century.

Far from feeling insecure about taking responsibility for tens of thousands of workers at such a young age, Philippe was happy that finally he could do his job without having to ask for permission to carry out certain projects. Every morning he went to different areas of the excavation to evaluate the contractors' progress. Then he'd visit patients at the nearest hospital who were sometimes cared for out in the open for lack of space.

So not to lose time, Philippe ate stew for lunch in the workers' mess hall and then returned to the excavation to study the enemy: he spent hours trying to understand the various types of terrain they'd have to dig into.

At night, he'd joint his subordinates to discuss the progress of the work for which each was responsible. At ten at night, he would read and write letters or reports for the office in Paris. He'd sleep three hours before beginning a new day. He'd never been so tired, but he'd also never been so happy.

French dredge during excavations.
Photo Courtesy: Panama Canal Authority

6

January 1886

"Finally de Lesseps is coming!" Philippe thought when he finished reading the cablegram. In six weeks the Chambers of Commerce of several countries would be arriving to check the progress of the project. "Things must be very bad..." he thought when he realized that the true purpose of the visit was to try to convince businessmen from the United States, Germany, England, and other countries to invest in the Canal Company.

During the following weeks, all of Panama prepared for the second coming of "Le Grand Français", who would be accompanied by his son, Charles, vice president of the company headed by his father. Streets were cleaned, buildings were painted, and activities were planned to entertain a delegation of more than one hundred people. Large amounts of wine and food were imported especially for the celebration. Philippe did his best to have reports, graphs, and discussions ready to impress de Lesseps.

On the afternoon of February 17, the young general director of the company in Panama anxiously awaited the arrival of the visitors. With his uniform impeccably pressed and his now mature mustache perfectly waxed, the young engineer observed as the steamship Washington neared the pier. Once it had docked, to Philippe's delight, the first person to come down the ship's stairway was Ferdinand de Lesseps.

"Mr. President, I'm Philippe Bunau-Varilla, general director of the project. Welcome to Panama," he said nervously. "Le Grand Français" extended his hand to Philippe and spoke slowly and deliberately, "Ah, yes, Mr. Bunau-Varilla. I have received your reports. Thank you, thank you so much." And without another word, his idol continued to greet the rest of the engineers and local dignitaries who had come to receive him. The patriarchs from the Obaldía, Boyd, Arango, and Arosemena families, among others welcomed the affable visitor while the rest of the delegation disembarked from the ship and the military group from the American gunboat Galena, courtesy of admiral Jouett, played upbeat melodies.

As the visitors finished greeting the reception committee, Dr. Amador gave each a small box of quinine pills to protect against tropical illnesses, and *Bursera simaruba*, an antidote for venomous snake bites. Philippe enjoyed watching the horror on the guests' faces as they read the instructions written on the tiny papers inside the small first aid kits they had received.

That night a welcome supper was served at the Gran Hotel. The dinner, Panama's most important event of the year, was prepared by French and Italian chefs brought in specifically for the occasion, and accompanied by a large quantity of *Mouton Rothschild, Beajoulais, Chianti Classico* and *Frescobaldi* to make the dancing to follow all the more enjoyable. After speeches by local dignitaries, and at the request of Ferdinand de Lesseps, the celebration lasted until dawn.

Big reception for Count Ferdinand de Lesseps during his second visit to Panama in 1886. Public domain image.

The following weeks were full of activities for the visitors. Each morning at seven o'clock sharp, the groups went off to observe different areas of the project. They went to the Culebra Cut, the hospitals, workers' dorms, Matachin, the Chagres River, and Panama City, and were always accompanied by engineers who optimistically explained the progress of the work. Philippe had chosen to lead the group which included Ferdinand de Lesseps and the American committee.

On one of the site visits, the general director blew up a small mountain along the excavation route, to the delight of the visitors. That night, Philippe handed to de Lesseps, with great ceremony, a small rock that represented one thousandth of a millionth of the mountain he'd blown up that morning.

Despite the success, or at least, the hopefulness resulting from having the visitors to Panama, Philippe was frustrated because he hadn't managed to sit down and talk, not even once, with his idol. Each time he tried to get near, for some reason "Le Grand Français" had something else to do. Philippe didn't understand why de Lesseps was keeping his distance.

***

One afternoon, while the guests were resting after an excursion to the island of Taboga, Ferdinand de Lesseps asked Philippe to call together available engineers to discuss some technical details. Once everyone was in the Canal Company offices, they were seated around a large table to listen to what de Lesseps had to say. It was at this moment that Philippe understood the attitude of "Le Grand Français."

"Mr. Bunau-Varilla, I have received reports that you are proposing to change the design of the canal in order to incorporate locks. From the beginning I have said that this was to be a sea level canal, as in Suez, without locks. "Is this rumor true?" the patriarch asked, obviously irritated.

"Mr. President, this is one of the things I'd been hoping to discuss with you, but haven't had the chance. If you prefer, we could talk later so I could explain…"

"Now, please," de Lesseps said firmly.

Philippe cleared his throat before proceeding, and thought about his answer for a fraction of a second before responding confidently, "Several years have passed since we began the work here in Panama. Now we are more familiar with the geology of the land we are excavating and I believe a canal at sea level would be rather expensive. If we make it with locks, we can open the canal in less time. If we combine the locks with the creation of an artificial lake, as Godin de Lépinay suggested some years ago, we would significantly reduce the total excavation and we could open the canal sooner…"

"Of course. So the young engineer knows more than all of the members of the technical committee. Right?" de Lesseps replied sarcastically.

"No, Mr. President. But considering that we now know that the land we are excavating is different from what we initially thought, we ought to adjust our plans accordingly. For example, the Lavalley machinery worked well in the sands of Egypt, but it doesn't work for excavating the rocky Panamanian land," Philippe said firmly but respectfully.

Ferdinand de Lesseps sat quietly, but his eyes betrayed a fury provoked by the junior engineer. Just then, one of the new recruits who had come with de Lesseps stepped in. His name was León Boyer, a distinguished graduate of the Polytechnic School that had become famous for constructing bridges throughout Europe.

Boyer remembered Philippe from his days as a student. "Philippe, we've been told that the Canal Company is restricting entry into the hospital to certain workers, and that some have been forced to die in the street. What can you tell us about this?"

Philippe answered without hesitation, "Mr. Boyer, this enterprise isn't a charity institution. It is true that the hospital is denying entrance to several people, but only because they aren't really ill. Go to the hospital and you will see that eighty percent of the patients are black natives of the French Antilles. Since they were freed from slavery, they've devoted their lives to being professional patients. Then go to the excavation site. There you will find that eighty percent of the blacks working are Jamaican."

"Are you insinuating that Anglo-speaking blacks are better workers than French-speaking blacks?" Boyer asked incredulously.

"Mr. Boyer, I'm not insinuating—I'm telling you. You need only visit the excavation site and the hospitals to confirm that what I'm saying is the truth," Philippe stated firmly.

Boyer's questions and the questions of other engineers continued and Philippe answered with authority, demonstrating absolute knowledge of the operation. Even though the technical personnel seemed to understand and accept Philippe's explanations, Ferdinand de Lesseps remained clearly displeased with the young man's arrogance.

Ferdinand de Lesseps during his second visit to Panama; the girl seated on the stairs is his daughter. Philippe is standing sideways on his left. Photo courtesy of Mr. Ricardo López Arias.

7

One night, after another banquet in honor of the guests, and when the date of their departure was approaching, Philippe sat beside de Lesseps who was enjoying a glass of wine while watching the people dance.

"Mr. de Lesseps, I'd like to ask your opinion on what you've seen here in Panama. I know that some members of the committee are worried because of my age, but I believe that the results of my actions speak for themselves. For the first time we have managed to exceed the monthly excavation goals, we have imposed more order in the operations, and we have improved relations with the Americans. I…"

Shushing him with a raised hand, and without looking at him, de Lesseps said, "Yes, Mr. Bunau-Varilla, you really have managed to do an excellent job for the past few months. But now it's best that you leave this in more… experienced hands. Furthermore, your two-year contract has ended and you deserve a vacation. I have appointed León Boyer to take over your position as general director in Panama as of this week. We thank you for all your hard work and please assist Boyer in the transition process. As for now, enjoy the party."

Without giving Philippe a chance to finish what he had intended to say, the old man got up and with his glass of wine in hand, went to dance. Philippe couldn't breathe; he was shocked and ashamed as his eyes dampened with anger and frustration. He got up and went outside to get some air.

As he watched the people celebrating in the plaza, he was trying to control himself when someone tapped him on the shoulder, "*Romeo y Julieta*, Mr. Bunau-Varilla?"

Turning to look up, he recognized John Bigelow, American diplomat and businessman who had come as a representative of the New York Chamber of Commerce. Tall and thin, he wore his sideburns exceptionally long while his beard and mustache were cleanly shaven. His disheveled hair framed a face that could effortlessly pass from grave to cordial. In his large hand, he held out a Cuban cigar, "Would you like a *Romeo y Julieta*, Mr. Bunau-Varilla?"

"Good evening, Mr. Bigelow. Yes, thank you very much," Philippe answered, still in a daze as he lit the cigar. On various occasions he had spoken with the refined gentlemen who always had several questions during his visits to the site.

"It's a peculiar situation, isn't it, Mr. Bunau-Varilla?" Bigelow asked.

"Excuse me, I don't understand. What are you talking about?"

Blowing a puff of smoke, the vibrant seventy-something looked toward the plaza before he continued, "Everyone knows that the Canal Company is on the verge of bankruptcy. Soon the money will be gone and they will have to suspend the excavation. They still don't know what to do about the Chagres River, the excavation of the Culebra Cut has been sluggish, they haven't been able to contract enough laborers, and diseases are killing the few workers they do have.

Bigelow paused for a moment to watch the reaction of the young French engineer, who was looking back defiantly, all the while knowing that the American was telling the truth. "Still, despite the evident financial crisis of the Canal Company, you've spent a fortune in bringing us here and entertaining us with a grand show. All intended to convince us to invest our money for you to manage. Rather contradictory, don't you think?"

Philippe hesitated and finally responded, "Mr. Bigelow, I assure you that the company is very well-managed…"

Looking satisfactorily at Philippe, Bigelow interrupted, "Yes, Mr. Bunau-Varilla, I know that you have achieved a lot in a short amount of time. But that isn't enough. There is too much bureaucracy, too much corruption in the Canal Company. Or at least, that's what they tell me in Paris."

"You know people in Paris, Mr. Bigelow?" Philippe asked,

immediately regretting the naïveté of his question.

"You could say that. I had the honor of serving President Lincoln as ambassador to Napoleon III. I was the one who gave him the choice to leave Mexico or entering in a war with the United States. But that's in the past. Now, more importantly, I want to ask you, Mr. Bunau-Varilla, why are you here?" Bigelow savored his Cuban.

"To carry out my duty to France. To complete the canal," Philippe responded immediately, and followed with a summary of the changes he had proposed that very morning in order to ensure that the project progressed more quickly. Bigelow was intrigued by the fierce intelligence of the young engineer and his passion to complete the canal.

"It's clear, Mr. Bunau-Varilla, that the Panama Canal will be completed one day. In spite of the actual problems, there has been progress and too much has been invested to consider abandoning the project. Still, the financial disaster and the obstinacy of your boss will eventually bankrupt the Canal Company," Bigelow said.

"And another country will assume financial control, just like what happened with England and the Suez Canal..." Philippe responded sadly.

"Probably so." Taking note of the lost look on Philippe's face, the American asked, "Let's see, Mr. Bunau-Varilla, from what you tell me, advancement of the excavation depends on the contractors changing the way they work. But at the same time, you explained to me that this won't happen because to do so would increase the contractor's costs. And finally, de Lesseps doesn't agree with your ideas and is going to replace you with someone more experienced?"

"That's correct, Mr. Bigelow."

"You know, once Abraham Lincoln told me that 'it isn't the years in your life that count; it's the life in your years,'" Bigelow said, still savoring his Cuban.

"I'm sorry Mr. Bigelow, but I don't understand."

With a generous smile, the businessman said, "It seems to me, Mr. Bunau-Varilla, that you have the ability, experience and passion necessary to make a large contribution to this Grand Idea, as you call it. But you are looking in the wrong place."

Philippe's face expressed his confusion.

"Mr. Bunau-Varilla, have you not considered leaving your position at the Canal Company and becoming a contractor for your former employer? Founding your own business, perhaps?" Bigelow said as he expelled another puff of smoke.

John Bigelow
Photo: United States Library of Congress

8

Paris, May 1886

"Brother, you still look bad," said Maurice Bunau-Varilla while enjoying a casserole of calf's head, which he loved. They were seated in the rear section of *Le Procope*, Maurice's favorite restaurant, when they began discussing business. Observing the pictures of former guests that hung on the walls, Philippe tasted his *coq au vin*, a dish he had longed for while in Panama. "Do you know that Mr. de Lesseps even came to tell our mother that you had died?"

"Yes, mother told me. I still feel weak. I never thought I would get yellow fever right before returning to Paris. Luckily it wasn't fatal, or you wouldn't have had the pleasure of inviting me to supper," Philippe smiled. He had lost weight and was very pale, but he hadn't lost his sense of humor.

The brothers had spent a lot of time together in the preceding weeks, during which Maurice told Philippe about his successful banking career and of his plans to marry Sonia de Brunhoff, his girlfriend of three years and the sister of an old school friend. Philippe was mostly interested in talking about the Panama Canal.

"Tell me about this business," Maurice said as he motioned to the waiter that they didn't need anything else at the moment.

Philippe sat up straight in his chair, "As I explained, the idea is to buy up the majority of the shares of a small contractor called *Artigue, Sonderegger & Co.*, or A.S., which is currently in charge of Bohío Soldado, retain the existing owners as minority partners, and then we will negotiate the rights to excavate the Culebra Cut. That's where the greatest opportunity is. You will stay here in Paris to manage A.S. billings to the Canal Company, and send us equipment and supplies. I will run the operations of A.S. in Panama."

"Aren't you worried about diseases? You almost died a few weeks ago..."

Philippe looked directly into his brother's eyes, "I'm not afraid, and that is the greatest defense."

Maurice nodded and smiled, leaned toward his brother and quietly said, "And why, my dear brother, would we be interested in buying a company in Panama when the majority of them are losing money?"

"Because I know how to make money in Panama, Maurice. The problem isn't in excavating the land, like everyone says. The problem is that they've been going about it the wrong way, trying to use methods that work in Europe or in Egypt while the land in Panama is completely different. The land on the Culebra Cut is unstable, but I know how to excavate it successfully," Philippe responded, clearly excited.

Maurice loved asking his brother questions about the project. "If the solution is so easy, why haven't the other contractors implemented the changes?"

"I didn't say it would be easy. When I made these recommendations to the contractors, they didn't accept them because at first glance, the cost is greater. But in the long run, we will be able to excavate more because we won't have to stop due to landslides. Furthermore, with A.S. we will be able to research even more efficient methods, such as using dynamite on the rock under water to break it down and in turn, we will be able to excavate with more ease..." Philippe was beginning to come alive again when his brother covered his ears in jest, asking Philippe to stop. Maurice wasn't interested in engineering—he was only concerned with the finances.

"And are you sure that the company that has the right to excavate Culebra will be willing to hand over their contract?" Maurice asked, now more interested.

Philippe's eyes lit up, "I have already spoken to the Anglo-Dutch Company. Their obligation is to excavate 700,000 cubic meters per month on the Culebra Cut and in four years they have barely managed to complete 100,000 per month. My offer was that they relinquish the contract to us, and in exchange, we would pay the original commission per cubic meter excavated. They accepted immediately."

"We're going to do the excavation and they will collect their original commission for not doing a thing? And how will we make any money?" Maurice exclaimed.

Philippe leaned back in his chair and responded satisfactorily, "The current contract is quite beneficial because all the equipment, trains, rails, and excavation machinery is supplied by the Canal Company. We simply have to pay the workers. And I am certain that we can renegotiate with Charles de Lesseps a more profitable contract. This afternoon I'm meeting with him to negotiate the terms, so you don't need to worry. What I want to know is if you will be my partner or not."

Maurice thought for a moment. "And your American friend will lend us the money to initiate the operation?"

"Yes, the funding is available as I said. I will run the operation in Panama. I only need you to take charge, from Paris, of the financial management of A.S. Will you be part of it or not?"

Maurice still wasn't ready to give an answer. "Everyone knows the Universal Company is going to burn out sooner or later. What happens if it goes bankrupt next month and we lose everything before we've even begun?"

Philippe was getting impatient. Moving his plate of sorbet aside and tapping the table with a closed fist to make his point, he responded, "The Canal Company isn't going to go bankrupt yet. We will make the most of this opportunity which is available right now. Will you be my partner, yes or no?"

Smiling, Maurice Bunau-Varilla got up to shake his brother's hand.

9

Culebra Cut, January 1887

The first thing Philippe did upon his arrival in Panama, now that he was no longer an employee of the Canal Company but rather, the manager of A.S., was to make sure a home would be built for him on a hill near the excavation. This way, he could more easily supervise his workers and save time not having to come from Panama City, which was where the rest of the contract company managers lived.

There was no time to lose: he had to excavate quickly in order to make money and in turn, pay the loan he'd received. Immediately, Philippe attacked the primary problem on the Culebra Cut: the landslides constantly brought the work to a halt. He had observed with frustration as the contractors became accustomed to hauling the rock and soil from the excavation by train to a nearby hill to be unloaded down the slope. When the discarded materials accumulated to a certain height, the railways extended to the edge of the new terrace so that debris could continue to be thrown downhill. The main problem with this process was that the land on which the rails were built was unstable and when it rained, it would inevitably collapse and take the railway with it. Unable to evacuate the excavation debris, the job couldn't progress until the rails were repaired.

Philippe had proposed several times that the contractors construct a system of wooden bridges so that the railways would have a solid foundation, but no one had been interested in taking his advice.

However, when the new company erected their bridges to evacuate the excavation debris and the rains came, there were no collapses that affected the progress of the job and in a short time A.S. extracted several times more cubic meters of debris than any other contractor on the isthmus.

The other major problem that had to be resolved, according to Philippe, was the employees' lack of commitment. Most of them were there for the substantial salaries, but from the insignificant progress that had been made, few of them believed the canal would ever actually be finished. A short time after the work had begun, and once he had identified certain workers to use as examples, Philippe fired two supervising engineers and made sure that the rest of the personnel were listening: "I don't care about your titles or past experience. To accept your salary without believing in the possibility of success is to betray everyone else. Not believing that we will complete the canal is reason enough to fire you!" And with that, all of the workers continued working with a newfound commitment.

And so, with a combination of Philippe's engineering skills and a strong-handed administration, along with Maurice's iron-fisted financial management in Paris, A.S. became the most successful contractor on the isthmus. They excavated five times as much as previously had been done, and managed, for the first time, to break through Culebra, a task which had seemed impossible.

Satisfied, Philippe watched as other companies began to copy his methods of excavation, and soon the entire project in Panama was progressing more quickly than ever. It was a time of great success for the Bunau-Varilla brothers, during which they amassed a large fortune which would last them the rest of their lives.

The end of this period of prosperity came when, after slow and painful agony for many small-time French investors, the Canal Company went bankrupt on February 4, 1889. Hundreds of thousands had lost all their savings because they had subscribed to the dream of Ferdinand de Lesseps, who, in a desperate attempt to breathe life into his enterprise, had tried to finance the continuation of the excavation by issuing new lottery bonds that, in the end, no one dared to buy.

Furthermore, some mysterious person sent a telegram to Parisian banks falsely announcing the death of de Lesseps, which drove away several potential investors and put an end to any efforts to revive the company.

When the order was given in Panama to stop the operation on May 15th of that year, A.S. closed their doors and its manager prepared for his return to Paris. For Philippe, it had been thirty productive months; a very satisfying time. He remembered only one bad day during his stay in Panama: the 13th of March, 1888. On that day, a cablegram had arrived from Maurice informing him that his beloved grandmother, Mamie, had passed away. Sitting in the mud during a heavy downpour, Philippe had cried inconsolably. On several occasions when he'd needed his mother but she wasn't there, Mamie had loved, protected, and cared for him. And when Mamie got sick and needed him, Philippe had been far away, in the middle of the Panamanian jungle.

Theodore Roosevelt Collection, Harvard College Library

Courtesy of the Theodore Roosevelt Collection, Harvard College
Library
(560.52 1906-061)

10

At almost the same time that the Canal Company had gone bankrupt, the Maritime Canal Company of Nicaragua had been created with an initial investment of one hundred million dollars and J.P. Morgan as its main shareholder. The object of this new enterprise was to give the United States control of the oceans by way of a canal conceived of by Americans, constructed by Americans, and controlled by Americans.

On his way back to Paris, Philippe had made two stops. The first for the purpose of getting to know the new enemy of his canal: Nicaragua. The purpose of the second stop was to visit Mr. Bigelow, with whom he had regularly corresponded since their visit in Panama.

In Nicaragua, the engineer visited the mouth of the San Juan River. He studied the banks on the Costa Rican side and the Nicaraguan side, riding along the sections that would be excavated, and then visited the stunning lake of Nicaragua. From there, he took a boat to the island of Ometepe, where he admired the beautiful inactive volcanoes and, even though it was very far from where the Nicaragua Canal was proposed to pass through, he also visited the Momotombo Volcano from Victor Hugo's "Legend of the Ages." During the month he was in Nicaragua, Philippe was enchanted by the beauty of the volcanic country and by the friendliness of its people. The engineer clearly observed that, as a country, Nicaragua was much more stable and peaceful than Panama, a political subject of Colombia.

But there was no mistake: Nicaragua was the enemy and the threat was clearly for the revival of the French canal. H.B. Slaven and other contractors had already begun to transport their engineers and equipment from Panama and the labor recruiters were already offering Jamaican laborers work at the "new canal." If Panama was going to triumph, Nicaragua had to lose.

When he was satisfied with the amount of information he had obtained in Nicaragua, Philippe traveled to New York where he would catch the steamer that would take him to France, but first he would visit Mr. Bigelow.

They had maintained a special relationship, like "father and son," according to Bigelow, and as "equals" the Frenchman thought. For several days, Philippe stayed at his host's mansion at 21 Gramercy Park in Manhattan, and the two of them held lengthy conversations on the topic of the Panama Canal.

"Even though, technically, Panama is a better route than Nicaragua, and on that I agree, the Panama Canal is dead, Philippe. Panama is too complicated—every year there is a new attempt at independence from Colombia. And poor management guarantees that no one will want to invest any of their money into it; and frankly, the simple fact that it's a French project makes it less attractive," Bigelow said. "If you are so sure that Panama is the best route, in spite of all that, you will have to convince a lot of people to change their minds. That will take time and money," the older man pointed out, seated on a sofa in his home's library.

"Fine, but it is possible to change the people's opinion. Correct? And that is your specialty, Mr. Bigelow. If you were in my place, what would you do?" Philippe asked.

Bigelow, clearly pleased, responded: "There are two routes. To many, the French already proved that one wouldn't work. To change that, you have to show, in a way that they will easily understand, why, in spite of the failure in Panama, it is still the best route. Again, it must be easy for them to understand because the people deciding are politicians and everyone knows they aren't that smart!" the older man said, smiling.

During the return voyage to France, from the steamship's deck, Philippe watched as the dolphins leapt along the side of the ship while he thought about all of his mentor's recommendations. "Mr. Bigelow has a point. It makes sense to write a book demonstrating the advantages of Panama over Nicaragua and how we should complete the construction."

That night, in the comfort of his first class cabin, Philippe began writing the first of many books destined to promote the Grand Idea. He would call it, "Panama: Past, Present, and Future."

Canal route--Ometepe volcano and Lake Nicaragua from boat landing, San Jorge, Nicaragua, C. A. (Cropped image.)
Photo: United States Library of Congress

11

Paris, May 1889

From the time that Philippe returned to France, he and his brother had spent all their time liquidating everything related to their business in Panama. Both of them were aware that they had earned plenty of money with their enterprise, but neither of them was sure of the exact amount. The accountants in Maurice's office had spent only fifteen days in determining the financial situation and when they presented their findings, the brothers couldn't believe their good luck.

In just over two years, they had accumulated a fortune of almost fifteen million francs and had no debts. The company had been so profitable that their only loan had been paid off in the first six months of operation. The Bunau-Varilla brothers had excavated more than any other contractor of the Canal Company and, within their contract, they had managed to negotiate a large number of performance bonuses which they collected without any trouble. Also, Maurice accounted for a number of fines that had resulted in additional profits. For example, if one of the machines broke down for any reason, A.S. could fine the total cost to the Canal Company to compensate for their losses.

Finding themselves in possession of such splendid capital, Maurice began to explore various investment options. Philippe, on the other hand, wondered how he could use his new fortune to help Ferdinand de Lesseps finish the canal. "Forget about the canal—it's a lost cause. Half of France lost their money and no one is going to want to put their money on de Lesseps again," Maurice said, tired of his brother's foolishness.

In investing their share of the loot, each brother had his own preference. Maurice wanted to invest in a newspaper or buy properties and he already had a few options in mind. Philippe wanted to start a new company and hire the engineers who had worked with him in Panama. But for several months, they didn't settle on any investment in particular and took advantage of the time to enjoy their new fortune.

Philippe bought a recently constructed mansion on *Avenue d'Iena* which had been designed for a large family. Since Maurice had been caring for their mother for the past few years, Philippe invited her to live with him. This also allowed Maurice a bit of privacy since he had recently married his girlfriend Sonia.

"You should marry Ida. You're thirty years old now and plenty rich. It's time to start a family. And it's convenient," Maurice said. Even though Philippe had never been interested in Sonia's sister, his older brother had always given him good advice. And so, after a brief courtship, Philippe and Ida de Brunhoff were married that summer. Happily for the new couple, Ida gave birth to their first son, Etienne, on May 10, 1890, who was followed two years later by a vivacious daughter named Giselle.

Things couldn't have been better for the Bunau-Varilla brothers: young, rich, and ambitions, they had a promising future ahead of them. And things continued this way for a few years...

Until January 1892, after an opulent supper at *Foyot* restaurant, when both couples were leaving the establishment to get into their carriage, several people stood on the sidewalk before them and shouted, *"Panamistes!"*

Surprised and frightened by the famous epithet coined by Édouard Drumont for the "thieves of Panama," Maurice and Philippe swept their wives away as fast as they could and fled to their respective homes.

Recently purchased home of Philippe Bunau-Varilla, at Avenue
D´Iena.
Courtesy of Philippe Bunau-Varilla family

Édouard Drumont was convinced that all of France's problems
originated from the same source: Jews. The fear-provoking journalist
had become famous for his book, *La France Juive*, and now shocked
the public through his newspaper, *La Libre Parole*, in which he
demanded, on a daily basis, justice for all the small investors who had
lost their savings when they put their trust in Ferdinand de Lesseps.

The elderly de Lesseps, who had also lost all his money and who
had honorably tried to help with the liquidation process of the
Panama Canal Company, suddenly found himself accused by
Drumont of having conducted a large-scale fraud in collusion with
Jewish financiers.

"This criminal is treated like a hero, while the poor devil who
steals a loaf of bread is dragged to court like an animal. But in the
case of the Panama Canal, where over a billion francs were lost, most
of them from working-class families, no one has ever asked de
Lesseps, "What did you do with the money?" wrote Drumont.

The public's response was so great that the Minister of Justice,
Louis Ricard, requested an audit of the Panama Canal Company's
accounts. In October, criminal charges were brought against
Ferdinand de Lesseps and Gustave Eiffel, among other notable
French businessmen; soon newspapers were reporting that their

houses and offices had been searched by police.

When word of the raids spread, the majority of former contractors for the Canal Company were justifiably worried. At that moment, Maurice said to Philippe, "They'll be coming for us soon, brother." From that point on, political strife grew and worsened until one morning *Le Temps* newspaper reported that Baron Jacques de Reinach had committed suicide.

"Shit!" thought Philippe. When he couldn't reach an agreement with Charles de Lesseps to give them the excavation contract for the Culebra Cut, Maurice had said he would go through Baron de Reinach in order to convince de Lesseps. A few days later, a triumphant Maurice returned to report that not only had he secured the Culebra Cut, but he'd also negotiated other sections of the excavation for their new company, A.S. Philippe preferred not to ask how his brother had achieved this; the reputation of de Reinach and the audacity of Maurice didn't allow for any doubts.

12

Paris, October 1892

"Welcome to France, Mr. Loomis, it's a pleasure to meet you. Mr. John Bigelow wrote advising me of your transfer; I want you to know that I am at your service for anything you may need," Philippe said as they walked into the enormous library in his Paris home.

Like Philippe, Francis Loomis had found in John Bigelow a mentor with whom he could regularly correspond and who had helped him in forming his professional career. Tall, thin, elegantly dressed and with a penetrating gaze, Loomis was a few years older than Philippe. When he went to take a seat, he stopped before a colorful portrait of his host that hung on the wall. "What an interesting use of color! If you don't mind my asking, Mr. Bunau-Varilla, who painted this?"

Philippe got up and walked across the Persian rug to where his guest was standing. "An artist named Paul Gauguin. He came to Panama to paint, but things didn't go as planned for him and after a short while, he had run out of money. He had a strong build so when he came asking for work, we contracted him." Smiling as he recalled the scene, he added, "It was interesting to see him there among the workers, like a grain of white rice among an army of ants."

Without taking his eyes off the painting, Loomis asked, "And after the excavation ended, did Gauguin stay in Panama?"

"I don't think so. One day he was arrested for urinating in the middle of the street. I bailed him out of jail and offered some money for steamship tickets so he could leave the isthmus. In thanks, he painted this picture of me before he left. Actually, his use of color seems rather peculiar to me, but I like it," Philippe said, signaling for his guest to have a seat beside him at the fireplace.

"Very impressive. I love his style," Loomis said, making himself comfortable.

"So, Mr. Loomis, I understand that you will be serving as consul in *Saint Etienne*. But in his letter, Mr. Bigelow said that you recently joined diplomatic service. If you don't mind my asking, what did you do before?" Philippe asked as he accepted a cup of coffee from the attending servant.

"I met Mr. Bigelow working as a reporter for the *New York Tribune*; he encouraged me to get into the public sector, and prior to this appointment, I was a librarian for the state of Ohio. Mr. Bigelow tells me that you two met in Panama." And with that comment, Philippe launched into his favorite topic.

For an entire hour he told Loomis about how the Canal Company had been shut down just when they had finally managed to solve several technical problems that would allow them to progress more efficiently. "I recommended we abandon the idea of a sea-level canal and construct one with locks, but once my recommendations were accepted, it was already too late..." Philippe lamented.

"It's too bad about what happened in Colombia, Mr. Bunau-Varilla. The good thing is that even though the location will be different, the United States will build the interoceanic canal," Loomis said, affirming that the Nicaraguan route was indeed better. Which led to Philippe taking another hour to explain to his guest the advantages of Panama over Nicaragua.

"My dear Mr. Loomis, to choose Nicaragua over Panama is to choose the unstable route over the ideal route. That of Panama is three times shorter, and will cost less to build and maintain. Furthermore it isn't affected by marine winds or currents. Nicaragua, on the other hand, is plagued by volcanoes that could destroy the interoceanic canal at any moment," Philippe self-assuredly pointed out. Recently, he'd received a letter from H.B. Slaven in Nicaragua and the postage stamp had caught his attention for its beautiful depiction of the Momotombo Volcano. Recalling his visit to Nicaragua, Philippe decided to add volcanoes to his growing list of weaknesses of the Nicaraguan route compared to the Panamanian.

"In addition, according to my friends in Central America, it looks like the Maritime Canal Company of Nicaragua will soon go bankrupt as well. So that should level the playing field a bit between the two routes!" Philippe said with a chuckle.

The passion with which Philippe spoke about the Panama Canal made quite an impression on Loomis, "Well, Mr. Bunau-Varilla, I see that Mr. Bigelow wasn't exaggerating when he said that you are the greatest advocate for the Panama Canal. It's a shame what has happened to Mr. de Lesseps and to his company. Truly a shame that it was all in vain..."

With a smile, Philippe corrected his guest, "You are mistaken, Mr. Loomis. Nothing has been in vain: the Panama Canal will be completed."

Portrait of Francis B. Loomis.
Photograph: "Panama, the creation, destruction, and resurrection" by
Philipe Bunau-Varilla.

13

Paris, April 24, 1894

It was a beautiful spring morning and Maurice Bunau-Varilla was enjoying the view from his new office at *Le Matin*. Even though he had intended to buy a larger and more successful newspaper, *Le Matin* was characterized by great quality and reliability. Maurice only had to find a way to increase circulation so his investment would yield greater profits.

"Excuse me, Mr. Bunau-Varilla, there are gentlemen here who need to speak to you," said one of his assistants from the door.

So pleased by the glorious morning he was appreciating from his window, Maurice didn't think to ask who was looking for him. "Miss Demarle, if it's urgent, send them in!" he said, still smiling and still looking out the window.

Just then, Maurice heard several footsteps approaching his door. When he turned around to see his visitors, his smile immediately disappeared. Accompanied by Miss Demarle were two dismal figures: one was a policeman and the other was surely a lawyer. Without even a hello, the lawyer declared, "Maurice Bunau-Varilla, I'm here to represent Mr. Lemarquis. I hereby deliver this notice which states that you are required to pay the sum of seven million francs immediately or face the consequences."

"And, why am I to pay such a sum? Of what are you accusing me?" Maurice inquired.

"You and your associates at the company *Artigue, Sonderegger &*

Co., or A.S., as it is also known, are accused of embezzling from the Panama Canal Company. I recommend that you pay back the money soon, Mr. Bunau-Varilla, if you want to avoid prison," the lawyer said firmly before turning and walking away.

14

Paris, August 1894

Philippe anxiously smoked his Cuban while waiting to be invited inside. Loyalty to his brother and self-interest in protecting his own name had brought him to this point. Even though he hadn't been accused, since his name didn't appear in the register of shareholders for *Artigue, Sondregger & Co.*, he requested permission to participate as a witness in a trial feared by many influential men, and for good reason. All of the principal contractors from the Canal Company had been equally accused.

Pacing up and down the hallway, Philippe wondered who the imbecile was who thought to discredit Maurice and his associates. It should have been clear to all of France that if it hadn't been for them, the Canal Company would have ceased to exist much sooner. France should have been thanking them, not condemning them.

The book that Philippe published in 1892, the ads he had taken out in the newspaper to generate support for the Grand Idea, and his constant pleas for France not to abandon construction of the canal, without a doubt caught the attention of the French National Assembly and the lawyer for all the small investors, as well as Mr. Lemarquis, and Mr. Brunet, the liquidator.

For an instant, he thought he'd made a mistake in making so many demands on France to never give up, but he immediately corrected himself: he would do it again a thousand times if it would help the canal to be completed.

Turning to pass back through the hallway, Philippe heard a door open and saw an usher leaning toward the opposite end of the building. When the usher turned back and saw Philippe, he gestured for the young man to come: it was time to testify.

Philippe entered the Chamber of Deputies, which was full of people; after bowing respectfully to be introduced and sworn in, he sat in the center of the gallery, right in front of the investigative committee. On his left, he saw Lemarquis whisper something to a colleague seated next to him.

The lawyer stood up, walked toward where Philippe was sitting, and without looking up from the paper in his right hand, asked, "Mr. Bunau, is it true that when you were general director of the Panama Canal Company, you had prostitutes on the payroll?"

Shocked by the question, it took Philippe a few seconds to recover and then to think about how to answer. "Mr. Lemarquis, you have to understand the context of the excavation in order for me to effectively answer your question. Remember that in Panama we had thousands of men in the middle of the jungle who needed to entertain themselves…"

Lemarquis didn't stop, "Mr. Bunau, I didn't ask if in Panama there were entertainment options. I asked if the Canal Company had prostitutes on the payroll. I will ask you again. Did the company pay for the services of prostitutes?"

Without moving a muscle or lowering his gaze, Philippe answered, "There were many problems in recruiting sufficient laborers for the excavations. The offices in Paris asked us to do everything possible to generate entertainment for the workers. But I have no knowledge of prostitutes being paid with the Canal Company's money."

Lemarquis continued looking at Philippe with a smug grin, "It is strange that during the time you were general director, you didn't notice payments to La Constancia, the most popular brothel in Panama."

"The Canal Company made thousands of payments each week, Mr. Lemarquis. I don't remember having any obligations to that establishment."

The liquidator observed Philippe, who challenged the lawyer with his gaze. After reshuffling his papers, Lemarquis continued,

"Mr. Bunau, we all know that the Canal Company lied about the number of deaths due to tropical diseases so not to generate fear among investors and also to avoid any problems in securing enough workers."

"I wasn't in charge of the Canal Company's reports, Mr. Lemarquis. I'm sure that you can find the people responsible for..."

"I haven't gotten to my question, Mr. Bunau," the lawyer interrupted, smiling. "Many workers in Panama were immigrants without any family or acquaintances who could claim the bodies..." When he said this final word, Lemarquis leaned toward Philippe, inviting him to speak.

"And?" Philippe said, unfazed.

"What do you know about the thousands of worker's dead bodies that were never claimed? What did the Canal Company do with the bodies?" Lemarquis barked.

"Mr. Lemarquis, there is no need for that tone. I will explain to you what you probably already know: many corpses were placed in barrels, one in each barrel, but sometimes with the Chinese, two bodies were placed in one barrel to save on freight. They were preserved in vinegar to later be sold to medical schools in various countries. The railroad initiated the sale of cadavers, and when it became a part of the Canal Company, we never changed making the sales. It's a completely legal practice."

Lemarquis pretended to be disgusted. "I don't doubt that it's legal, but is it moral, Mr. Bunau? I suppose that all depends on your point of view. But please, continue. What happened to the money earned through the sale of cadavers?"

"Those cadavers helped several medical schools to better prepare their students," Philippe protested.

"What happened to the money earned through the sale of the dead bodies of workers who were tricked into working in Panama?" the lawyer insisted.

Philippe understood that he wasn't going to convince Lemarquis. "It was recorded in the business accounts under 'other income.'"

As he read his notes, Lemarquis walked in circles, reminding Philippe of the circling vultures in Colón. "Mr. Bunau, you were general director of the Panama Canal Company. You then resigned to become manager of your brother's company, which mysteriously obtained the contract for the Culebra Cut, the most profitable excavation part of the entire project…"

"Culebra is the most dangerous and difficult part of the canal to dig. Two large companies had failed on it before we came. But thanks to our work, in a short time we managed to do five times more excavating than was previously accomplished. Our job…" Philippe stated emphatically.

Lemarquis interrupted again, "Now that you mention your job…What can you tell me about the contracts that your brother negotiated? The excavation goals were lowered to receive bonuses more quickly… How is it that the contracts were for the excavation of nine million cubic meters and, even though you only managed to excavate 2.6 million, you still received generous grants for your work?"

"Well, that was stipulated in the contracts…"

Lemarquis walked toward the desk where his documents were and leaned against it, crossing his arms. "Mr. Bunau, as manager of *Artigue, Sonderegger & Co.*, did you ever charge twice for the same excavation? For example, if a landslide forced you to transport debris, did you charge for that move as if it were another excavation?"

"All charges were according to the agreements in the contracts…"

Lemarquis left his papers on the desk and walked to meet Philippe. The eighty-four people in the room were paying close attention to every detail.

"Mr. Bunau, how do you explain that your brother, a bank employee, and you, a student on a scholarship to the Polytechnic School, were able, within two years, to accumulate enough capital to buy a newspaper, and invest in properties, railways, and mining businesses in Africa and Spain? What is your secret?"

Philippe, for the first time in his recollection, couldn't answer a question. He tried to say several things, but not one word would come out of his mouth.

Lemarquis smiled. "Since you can't explain, Mr. Bunau, allow me to do it for you. You took the knowledge you had gained as general director of the Canal Company to later negotiate unfair contracts with your former employer. And in this way, your brother and associates became very rich. But as you said before, Mr. Bunau, none of that is illegal. However, it is, indeed, immoral."

Confused and ashamed, Philippe was only able to utter, "My last name is Bunau-Varilla, not Bunau..."

Smiling, Lemarquis corrected himself. "Excuse me, Mr. Bunau-Varilla, I forgot that your mother, Caroline Pamela Bunau, had changed your name before you graduated from the Polytechnic School. No more questions."

And with that, Lemarquis ended his line of questioning. That night Philippe took refuge in his library, accompanied by a bottle of wine.

Ida, his wife, hadn't dared to ask how everything had gone. Philippe was furious and sad at the same time. Not because he knew that his participation in the trial had been a failure; and not because it had been costly for him to testify when he hadn't been obliged to do so. He was furious at that imbecile Lemarquis for daring to question him; he was sad that he couldn't remember the father he had never known.

15

Paris, October 1894

Five months had passed since Lemarquis accused A.S. of embezzlement, but still, nothing had been proven. Nevertheless, the brothers were anxious for the process to be over as soon as possible; so when Lemarquis summoned them to propose a settlement, Maurice and Philippe were happy to listen to his offer.

At the time, the liquidator of the Canal Company was preparing to begin a new enterprise: the New Canal Company. The machinery would break down if it was not used, so the objective was to keep the operation running at a minimum level in order to prevent further losses, until a permanent solution could be determined. The liquidator and his advisors had determined that the best possible solution was to sell the new company's assets, including the Colombian government's concession which allowed construction of an interoceanic canal in Panama.

As soon as Philippe heard the proposal, he urged Maurice to reject it. "To sell the assets and the rights from the Colombian government is to dishonor France! Absolutely not!"

"Philippe, are you crazy? Lemarquis accused us of stealing money from the Canal Company and you want to reject his plan to recover the investors' money?" Maurice had a point and Philippe had no other solution but to remain silent until they had reached an agreed upon negotiation with the liquidator.

Lemarquis needed working capital to be able to revive the

enterprise and maintain its operation. Once he had summoned all of the contractors accused of embezzlement, he revealed to them where the money was coming from. "Gentlemen, in exchange for dropping all charges against you, we are offering you to become the very first shareholders in the New Canal Company." At that, the faces of the attendees went white with shock.

"The amount that each individual is to invest will depend on the estimations we are currently disputing. It seems that the most convenient option is for you to accept our proposal and avoid further consequences." Once they understood how much money they would have to provide, all of them, including Gustave Eiffel, gladly accepted and immediately agreed to the proposition. For some reason, Lemarquis was asking for much less than before. And so, on the 24th of October, 1894, the New Panama Canal Company was founded.

During the first shareholders' assembly, the new Executive Committee was introduced, which came as a disagreeable surprise to Philippe. First because he hadn't been invited to participate in the committee, and second, because his former colleague in Panama, Maurice Hutin, had been elected president. "That coward won't accomplish anything."

The only novelty was getting to meet William Nelson Cromwell, the lawyer and representative for the Canal Company and for the railroad, which would continue operating as part of the enterprise still based in the United States. "Mr. Cromwell will represent us from his offices in New York and will be in charge of promoting the interests for the New Canal Company in the United States," Hutin said.

In spite of his prematurely gray hair and a look that betrayed egotism, Cromwell had a youthful face. He'd made himself a millionaire by reorganizing bankrupt businesses and then selling them. His clients included, among other powerful businessmen, J.P. Morgan, and he was known for having initiated an innovative practice known as "business lobbying" in the most prestigious political circles in the United States.

Upon their introduction, Philippe and Cromwell shook hands, one suspicious of the other. They were immediate, however reluctant, allies in the task of reviving the Panama Canal.

Portrait of William Nelson Cromwell.
Photo: Library of Congress, United States.

16

April 1895

France didn't have the money to finish building the canal alone: the government's priority was to invest in local infrastructure and the public didn't want to bet on the canal after the financial and political scandals that had discredited the project conceived by "Le Grand Français," who had died bankrupt the past December. His death was a great blow to Philippe, who had visited him several times at the country house where his elderly icon spent his final days. In spite of all that had happened in Panama, Philippe continued to admire him.

Walking near the Eiffel Tower one morning, thinking of ways to resuscitate the canal, Philippe remembered a conversation he'd had with Mr. Bigelow a few years back during his visit to Panama: France would need the support of an allied nation to be able to finish the canal.

It wouldn't be the United States—even after the Maritime Canal Company of Nicaragua went bankrupt a couple years ago, the U.S. maintained the idea of constructing their own canal in Nicaragua. Which other friendly country would be interested in joining France in the completion of the Panama Canal?

The answer was immediately resoundingly clear: Russia. That year, Russia and France had formed a political and military alliance. Russia was building the Siberian railway and could aid in the completion of the French canal in Panama. This would ensure the consolidation of a powerful alliance. Philippe got to work right away developing his idea.

Making use of his new fortune, he discovered that Prince Tatischeff was coming to Paris by train from Dortmund, Germany, and arranged to cross paths with him along the way. He would share a compartment with the prince. Upon entrance into the train car, Philippe awoke Tatischeff and then pretended not to know the man. "I'm sorry for having awakened you," Philippe said in terrible German.

Tatischeff responded in the elegant French spoken by Russian aristocrats and Philippe took the opportunity with which he'd been presented to strike up a conversation with the prince. By the end of the journey, the engineer had used his gift of persuasion to convince the prince to facilitate a meeting with the Finance Minister to the Tsar, Sergei Witte, with the purpose of discussing the Panama Canal.

A few weeks later, Philippe met with Minister Witte in Saint Petersburg.

In his office, the minister, taking a seat across from Philippe, asked, "Mr. Bunau-Varilla, you have come as a representative of the French government?" Witte was so tall that, even though both men were sitting, compared to Philippe, he appeared to be standing.

"No, Your Excellency, I don't represent the French government, nor do I work with the New Canal Company. I'm simply a patriot dedicated to the ideal the Panama Canal represents. France alone cannot complete the canal; we need our Russian brothers in order to finish the construction."

And with that introduction, Philippe took an hour to explain the plan that would solve all of the problems that had prevented completion of the canal thus far. The only thing missing was financial support from an ally nation to finish such a magnificent project. "Furthermore," said Philippe, "if Russia controlled the canal, it would have direct access to the Atlantic Ocean. A canal in Panama united to the Trans-Siberian Railway would allow the Tsar to control a large part of world commerce..."

After listening to Philippe's presentation, Minister Witte simply sat silently, looking into his eyes with an indecipherable smile. He appeared to be uncomfortable, and gave the impression he was censoring his thoughts to keep from speaking aloud. A minute passed and Philippe, unsure of what was happening, only managed to say, "What does Your Excellency think of our proposal?"

Witte stroked his beard with his right hand, smoothed his uniform and firmly began to speak, "Mr. Bunau-Varilla, we appreciate your visit but we aren't interested in your canal. France recently lent us 125,000,000 rubles that are essential here, in Russia... Do you think we are interested in spending the money we've borrowed on a dying enterprise? Thank you very much for your visit and have a pleasant journey back home." And without saying another word, the giant stood up, turned and headed for the office door.

Philippe remained seated, holding maps, diagrams, and charts full of statistics, not knowing what to do. He didn't understand what had just happened. Russia didn't want the glory of completing the canal? Russia didn't want to control naval traffic between the Pacific and Atlantic Oceans?

He only heard the minister's secretary say, "I will see you out, Mr. Bunau-Varilla. Follow me, please."

Sergei Witte, Russian Finance Minister
Photo: U.S. Library of Congress

17

Cuba, February 15, 1898

At 9:38 at night, Captain Charles Sigsbee was finishing a letter he was writing to his wife on the small desk in his cabin at the stern of the warship *U.S.S. Maine*. They had arrived at the port of Havana almost three weeks earlier to protect American interests from the worsening long-time conflict between Cuba and Spain.

"Soon I will be home, my love. The Spanish governor seems to have everything under control and there hasn't been any sign of the Cuban rebels for a few weeks now, so our presence probably won't be necessary for much longer," Sigsbee wrote, satisfied. "We have maintained excellent relations with the Spanish officials, who I invited to supper last week on the *Maine*. In return, they treated us to a bullfight, which I found a bit barbaric. But the Spaniards are all gentlemen and we've been treated kindly."

Sigsbee, with his mustache and white hair carefully parted down the middle, placed his round glasses on the table and put the letter in an envelope. Just then, an explosion sent him crashing to the floor. Dazed and deafened by the loud metallic sounds, he felt like the ship was sinking from the bow. Amid the darkness and smoke, he left his room and ran down the inclined corridor to where his men were, to try to save the ones he could before the ship went completely under.

The fire and water forced him back up to the deck. From there he watched as Havana lit up and it became clear to him what was happening... Soon he saw lifeboats from the Spanish ship *Alfonso XII* rowing toward the *Maine* to try to rescue the survivors. Over two hundred sailors, most of whom had been staying in the section that exploded, perished that night.

During the investigation to determine the cause of the tragedy, some of the survivors claimed to have heard several days prior to the explosion that the Spaniards were going to attack their ship. Motivated by the yellow press that for some time had been reporting on the supposed atrocities committed by the Spaniards against the Cuban people, the Americans sought revenge. A couple weeks later, Spain and the United States declared war against one another.

Unable to imagine at that time that this war would be of great importance for the Panama Canal, Philippe, like many others all over the world, attentively read how the U.S. Navy had ordered the American battleship *U.S.S. Oregon* to travel from San Francisco to Cuba. At top speed, the *Oregon* sailed from California to Peru, Chile, the Magellan Strait, Brazil, Barbados, and finally arrived in Cuba sixty-seven days after leaving San Francisco.

Aside from the Cuban war, the necessity for an interoceanic canal had once again been substantiated by the time it took for the *Oregon* to travel from one ocean to another. As a result, the American government revisited their interest in controlling an interoceanic canal. "Since the enterprise that was to excavate the Nicaragua Canal also went bankrupt, perhaps now the United States will want to support the Panama Canal..." Philippe mentioned to Maurice, who simply shrugged his shoulders and sighed at his brother's foolishness.

Photo # NH 46774 Diving on MAINE's wreck

Photo # NH 46765 MAINE funeral in Havana

Photos courtesy of the Navy History and Heritage Command of the
United States.

18

Caracas, Venezuela, June 1898

It was a very emotional time for Philippe, who saw the opportunity to resuscitate the Panama Canal. The United States had delayed in reviving the excavation of the Nicaragua Canal due to an argument between Senators Hepburn and Morgan over who would receive the honor of bequeathing his name to the project. Furthermore, the Costa Rican Congress had yet to decide whether or not to sign the treaty permitting the United States to construct the canal which would run through the San Juan River.

Taking advantage of an invitation to visit Venezuela from his friend, Francis Loomis, who had been named ambassador a few months ago, Philippe packed his suitcases to go back to Latin America. Once together, the two friends talked solely about the political situation in Colombia, and particularly about the war that was confronting liberals and conservatives all over the country. "They say the provinces of Cauca, Magdalena, and Bolívar also want to separate from Colombia," Loomis reported to his guest.

"Well, Panama tries to do it every year with no success..." Philippe joked.

Seated in comfortable rockers made of wood and leather, both of them enjoyed the wide corridor that looked out onto the garden of the United States Embassy. "Even if the Panama Canal is completed, it will always be affected by the instability of Colombia. It would be too risky for the United States to build the canal there, Philippe.

Roosevelt shares my opinion on the subject," Loomis pronounced, puffing on his pipe.

"Roosevelt?" Philippe asked.

"Until recently he was the Assistant Secretary for the Navy, but he left his position to enlist and fight in the Cuban war. Imagine, going to fight in a regiment composed entirely of volunteers when he could have been safe and sound in his office. Mark my words, Roosevelt will go far..." Loomis said excitedly.

But Philippe was only interested in one thing: "Well, back to the Canal; Panama is too risky as a part of Colombia, but if it were to gain independence, as it has been trying to do for several decades..." mused the engineer as he lit a Cuban and entertained the thought: "And if..."

Weeks later, Philippe would read that Colonel Theodore Roosevelt had requested that his superiors take the majority of the army off the island before they died, not from Spanish aggression, but from yellow fever and malaria.

19

New York, December 1, 1898

At the end of his visit to Venezuela, Philippe traveled to New York, where he stayed at Mr. Bigelow's house. Over the last two years, the Bigelow and Bunau-Varilla families had become friends, especially after Philippe invited the Bigelows to stay at his house in Paris where he acted as a splendid host. During this stay, he shared with Bigelow the plan he'd devised with Loomis in Venezuela. Save for certain recommendations made by the elder diplomat, which Philippe immediately accepted, the plan had been very well received.

Reticently, but following Bigelow's advice, Philippe visited William Nelson Cromwell, representative for the Canal Company in the United States, at his Manhattan offices to get him involved. "Mr. Cromwell, what we are about to discuss has to be treated with the utmost confidentiality," the French engineer stated before continuing, "We have a common goal, which is to see the Panama Canal come to fruition. If we work together, we can make this happen."

Philippe went on to propose to Cromwell that they unite forces so that the United States would abandon their plans to construct the Canal in Nicaragua and instead, acquire the assets of the Panama Canal Company. This sounded great to Cromwell, who was also a shareholder in the company.

Each of them would work in their area of expertise: Cromwell would discreetly lobby influential senators, especially Mark Hanna, and if possible, President McKinley. Philippe would try to convince as many American industrialists and businessmen as he could. He would present himself as a champion for Panama out of pure conviction, since he had no formal ties to the Canal Company. "Well, aside from the shares that Lemarquis obliged me to buy," Philippe said, in an unsuccessful attempt to break the ice.

Cromwell knew that no shareholder, not even the president of the Company, Maurice Hutin, had as much interest in the Panama Canal being completed as did this Frenchman. Something was motivating Bunau-Varilla tremendously, but William wasn't sure what that thing was. After all, what interested him was the commission he'd earn for selling the company and if he could get help doing that for free, perfect. So after a few meetings, Cromwell agreed to collaborate with Philippe and that's when their secret society began.

Across the city, from his office in Gramercy Park, John Bigelow, wrote a letter to his former assistant of many years. "Dear Mr. Secretary of State..."

John Milton Hay, who, after serving as secretary to Abraham Lincoln was sent to France as a diplomat, also had the honor of working for John Bigelow at that time. Writer of novels, devoted father and dedicated patriot, Hay highly respected the opinion of his venerable former boss.

The letter basically explained that, with all due respect, Bigelow wanted to share his suggestions for the secretary's consideration. Perhaps it was wise not to proceed with the plan to resurrect the Nicaragua Canal without first evaluating the opportunity presented by Panama. The progress in excavation made by the French couldn't be ignored and maybe it would be wise to put off continuing with Nicaragua until other options had been considered. Perhaps the French would be willing to sell the New Canal Company so that another country could finish the project?

Bigelow's involvement and the delay that had occurred in the Senate would allow President McKinley, in March of 1899, to be swayed by Bigelow and Cromwell to establish a new committee that would be responsible for evaluating both routes and recommending the better of the two. Members had been carefully selected by Cromwell, who, to Philippe's surprise, had abundant authority over certain influential politicians.

Consequently, the former Nicaraguan Canal Commission came to be called the Isthmus Canal Commission, avoiding attachment to a particularly named route. The new entity was commonly known as the Second Walker Commission in honor of Admiral John G. Walker, who would also lead this group. Panama was coming back to life.

By August of that year, the members of the new Commission would make their first exploratory trip to decide which route was better. But instead of going to Nicaragua or Panama, they would go to Paris.

20

Paris, August 1900

Philippe peeked into the window of the *Pavillon de l'Elysée* restaurant, which had recently been inaugurated on occasion of the Universal Exposition, and noticed Francis Loomis inside with his guests.

As he was accustomed to doing for as long as the Isthmus Canal Commission had been in France, Philippe took the opportunity to meet any visiting prominent Americans and give them his well-rehearsed "casual" presentation about the advantages of Panama over Nicaragua. This group in particular was attractive because it included various important businessmen who were also members of the influential Commercial Club of Cincinnati.

When he was sure that they were all seated, Philippe entered through the main door and signaled the host, who he handed a few bills, to be seated at a table for one near his friend. When Philippe passed by his table, Francis Loomis got up to greet him, "Philippe, what a coincidence! Allow me to introduce you to Mr. Watts Taylor and Mr. Harley Thomas Procter of Cincinnati, Ohio. This is Lieutenant Asher Baker and Mr. George Morison."

"Gentlemen, I'm pleased to meet you. Philippe Bunau-Varilla, at your service."

"Are you alone? Please, join us."

"I don't want to disturb you, gentlemen."

"Don't be silly, Mr. Bunau-Varilla. Any friend of Ambassador

Loomis is welcome at our table," Thomas Procter responded with a smile.

And so, Philippe dined with Loomis and his companions. Loomis mentioned that Philippe had been the general director of the Panama Canal Company, which allowed the engineer to take over the conversation for the next two hours, explaining to the visitors why Panama offered a better route than Nicaragua for building the canal.

"But, we didn't know a thing about this, Mr. Bunau-Varilla! You should come to Cincinnati and tell our friends everything you know! If Panama is a better route, French as it is—no offense to you!—the United States should consider it!" Procter exclaimed.

"Be careful if you visit, Mr. Bunau-Varilla, or Harley will sell you a mountain of Ivory soap to import to France!" Watts Taylor joked. The mood was light and all were enchanted by Francis Loomis' friend.

"Gentlemen, it would be an honor. I understand that Senator Mark Hanna is from Ohio, is that correct?" Philippe asked innocently.

"Of course, we know Mark very well. Perhaps he could join us if he's in Ohio. In fact, I think he's coming to Cincinnati in January…" Morison responded.

Philippe managed to be invited to speak to the most powerful senator in the United States about why the U.S. should choose Panama over Nicaragua as the location to build the American canal.

Harley Thomas Procter.
Photo Courtesy of the Procter & Gamble Company

21

Ohio, January 16, 1901

The invitation from the Commercial Club of Cincinnati had arrived on the 11th of December and by the 5th of January Philippe had boarded the steamship *Champagne* to America.

After several weeks of preparation, the moment had arrived when Philippe would explain to the United States why it was much better to build the interoceanic canal in Panama than in Nicaragua. From the podium, Philippe could see the auditorium full of Ohio's powerful businessmen and politicians, and among them was Mark Hanna.

The room was decorated with flags from France and the United States and, even though Philippe detected the audience's suspicions, he enthusiastically began his presentation, using the English he had perfected while living in Panama where he practiced daily with American military and engineers on the railway.

"Gentlemen, the interoceanic canal in Central America has been, for several countries, a centuries-old dream. But only the United States can make it a reality. The Monroe Doctrine demands it, and humanity needs it. During this session, I'm going to explain to you the progress that has been made in the construction of the Panama Canal; how we have overcome the most pressing problems; I will demonstrate why, technically speaking, Panama is a much better route than Nicaragua and I hope to be able to prove that, for the United States, Panama is a better option." The audience was impressed by the conviction with which the small Frenchmen spoke. His optimism and determination likened him to the American work ethic with which they were familiar.

For two hours, Philippe spoke about the advantages of the Panamanian route: a much shorter distance from ocean to ocean, fewer cubic meters to excavate, a lesser maintenance cost, and finally, Panama didn't have volcanoes while Nicaragua was plagued by them.

At the end of his presentation, the French engineer received a resounding applause. Satisfied, he saw that many of the faces that had appeared suspicious at the beginning of his lecture were now on his side. The first to approach him, limping and gasping from being overweight, was Senator Mark Hanna: "Mr. Bunau-Varilla, I am a simple mine operator. If I'm offered two mines and I can prove that one is better, I'm going to choose the one that is superior. You have convinced me: the United States deserves to build the Panama Canal."

That was the first of many presentations that Philippe gave in the United States; with the exception of New York, where he received a cool reception in *Delmonico's* restaurant, all of his audience members were convinced that Panama was the better route. Now he only had to convince the rest of the United States.

22

New York, November 1901

Philippe began to read the *New York Journal* and felt like the world was coming to an end: the Walker Commission had chosen Nicaragua as the best route to build the American canal.

He found himself alone, because Cromwell had been dismissed by the Canal Company a few months earlier for trying to create an American company to which the assets of the French enterprise would be transferred. The lawyer's plans had shocked his clients in Paris and naturally, generated a great deal of suspicion. While Philippe didn't care for the lawyer, his dismissal was a significant loss to the project.

The assassination of President McKinley the past September had caused a major setback for the Panama Canal. Little by little, McKinley had accepted the possibility of a canal in a location other than Nicaragua, if it were determined to be in the best interest of Americans. After McKinley's death, the young and fiery Theodore Roosevelt, who had recently been elected Vice President and who openly favored the Nicaraguan route, assumed the presidency of the United States.

The worst part was that, before announcing their decision, the Walker Commission made a formal request to buy the Canal Company, but Maurice Hutin and his friends hadn't wanted to put a price on it. Without an official price from the French, the Walker Commission had to estimate the price the Canal Company would request for its assets and this estimation turned out to be higher than the Nicaraguan expense.

In the end, the Walker Commission's report stated that technically, Panama was a better option, but that the estimated cost was too high and therefore, Nicaragua was the better route. In its evaluation, the Commission considered that the Canal Company franchise and its assets were hardly worth forty million dollars.

When Philippe, who had recently arrived in the United States, heard about this detail he took a steamer back to France to demand that the selling price be set at the forty million dollars determined by the Walker Commission. In a meeting of shareholders at the beginning of January, to which Philippe was entitled to attend, Maurice Hutin called out to him, "Philippe, for a Frenchman you make quite a fine American, wanting to give our assets to the United States with your proposal to accept that ridiculous sum."

As always, Philippe had anticipated such a reaction and he firmly responded, "Gentlemen! France won't be able to finish the canal alone, Russia can't help and the only country that has the ability and interest in continuing what he have begun is the United States. The Walker Commission already chose Nicaragua as the best option and all seems to have been lost. There is no other option. What is better, to lose some or to lose all? I will remind you of King Salomon when his tribunal ruled that the true mother was the one who would rather see her son in someone else's hands than to see him dead. That is the situation we are in. Now, decide!"

That day, Maurice Hutin was dismissed and the Canal Company sent an urgent cablegram from Paris to Admiral Walker confirming its willingness to sell everything for the forty million dollars that had been determined by the Commission, a price much lower than the cost estimated to build the canal in Nicaragua: 189 million dollars.

"This changes things…" Admiral Walker said, upon receipt of the lower offer from the French.

***

The news had hardly settled on Washington that the French had lowered the price to forty million dollars as requested by the Commission, when Mark Hanna, known for his innovative use of means of communication, issued a press release explaining that various "influential senators" were impressed by the technical advantages of Panama over Nicaragua and that, considering the new price Canal Company shareholders were asking, there was a possibility of changing plans in favor of the Panamanian route.

Politicians who were in favor of Nicaragua, headed by Senator Morgan, immediately took action. Reflecting on American public sentiment, ten days later the *New York Herald* published an article promoting the Nicaragua Canal as a national enterprise: a canal designed by Americans, built by Americans, and to be controlled by Americans.

On the 20th of January, almost three weeks after the French had sent their new proposal, President Roosevelt called on each member of the Walker commission to give him their opinion on the better route for the United States. It was obvious to all of them that now, for some unknown reason, Roosevelt preferred Panama. And so the Walker Commision changed their initial opinion and declared that Panama, not Nicaragua, was the best course.

But the Walker Commission's new declaration wasn't enough; the law that would allow the government to take possession of the canal and complete the construction had yet to be voted on. This entire process had caused a great deal of anxiety and depression for Philippe. He couldn't tolerate the fact that he had no control over what would happen, especially when it came to "his" canal.

23

Washington D.C., April 1902

"Brother, come with me to Cuba," Maurice announced upon entrance into Philippe's room at the New Willard Hotel. With his elegant suit and graying beard carefully clipped, Maurice didn't look a thing like his brother, who appeared haggard after not having left his room for a week. Philippe was so surprised by the visit that after affectionately greeting his brother, he was only able to utter, "What are you doing here? Why didn't you tell me you were coming? Why do you want to go to Cuba?"

"*Le Matin* wants to carry out an investigation of the advances in the fight against malaria and yellow fever. I decided that the best thing to do was to conduct the report myself, and since you know the tropics and speak Spanish, I want you to come with me," Maurice responded firmly.

"Maurice, I would love to go with you, but I can't. My friends need me here in Washington to…"

The older brother interrupted Philippe, "Your friends were the ones who asked me to come. They are worried, especially Mr. Bigelow. They say you've gone mad. Everyone knows you almost hit Mr. Morgan; and even the French embassy asked me to get you to come to your senses. Take a vacation, calm your nerves. You're putting everything you've worked for, for so many years, in danger."

The mention of Senator John Tyler Morgan brought Philippe back to reality.

A few weeks ago, he had gone to visit Mr. Morgan at his house to try to gain the senate's support for the Panamanian route. Bigelow, Cromwell, and his lawyer, Frank Pavey, had said that it was insane to try to persuade Morgan because the Nicaragua Canal had been the senator's signature project for decades, but nevertheless, Philippe went to the older gentleman's home.

From the very start, Morgan had provoked Philippe during his visit by calling him "Mr. Vanilla Bean" and then accusing him of being a swindler who wanted to sell "Panama trash" to the United States. The engineer had been so upset that he raised his fist to punch the senator. Even though Philippe restrained himself, Morgan's assistant had leaked the incident to the press.

Maurice finished earnestly, "Furthermore, it's good for you to dedicate a little time to our newspaper, which you seem to have forgotten in recent months. We'll leave in two days from New York on the steamer *Vigilancia*. Get ready," Maurice declared before leaving the room.

A few days later, the brothers found themselves on the island interviewing an American doctor who was trying to prove a notable theory: that yellow fever wasn't transmitted through filth, but rather, by certain types of mosquitoes.

"Actually, I am continuing the work begun by Dr. Carlos Finlay. We believe that other diseases such as malaria are also transmitted by mosquitoes," Dr. William Gorgas stated during his first interview with the Frenchmen.

The trip turned out as Maurice had hoped: the visits to the hospitals and conversations with Dr. Gorgas and his team piqued Philippe's scientific interests and helped him to relax. Little by little, the dark circles under his eyes were fading and his appearance was improving. Furthermore, he would be able to compose a very interesting report for his newspaper.

During one of the conversations, Philippe was torn between the excitement of learning a transcendental truth and the horror of what it meant: "But, Dr. Gorgas! If what you're saying is true, now we are aware of a significant cause for the failure of the Canal Company. In the hospitals, we would place small receptacles of water at the feet of the beds so that the ants wouldn't climb up and bite the patients. And it was in the water where the mosquitoes reproduce—we were helping to propagate the disease in the exact place in which we were trying to cure it!"

Dr. Gorgas replied, "Sadly, it's true. If we eliminate the places where mosquitoes reproduce and prevent them from biting people during the night with mosquito nets, for example, we can reduce the spread of diseases."

Watching the burning Cuban between his right thumb and index finger, Philippe smiled sadly. "And to think that I began smoking in Panama to keep bothersome insects away. I never thought it would help to protect me from diseases..." And with his tone falling sullenly, "If we had known this a few years ago, the canal would already have been completed..."

Gorgas replied quickly, "And thousands of lives would have been saved. But the good thing is that now when the construction of the Nicaragua Canal begins, we can avoid more deaths there."

The mention of the mortal enemy livened Philippe, "No, Dr. Gorgas, your knowledge will be of great use in Panama, where the United States will finish construction of the interoceanic canal."

Maurice only managed to smile at seeing Philippe in strong spirits again. A few days later, the Bunau-Varilla brothers returned to the United States, tired, excited, and one of them ready to face the United States Senate, and the other, the administration of their many enterprises.

24

Washington D.C., May 1902

Since the United States Congress has a bicameral system, it was of vital importance that the senate approved the Panamanian route before the House of Representatives held their respective election. If the senate chose Nicaragua in the first round of voting, Panama stood the chance of losing all together.

Philippe needed help. The French Embassy didn't want to intervene, the Canal Company heads didn't seem to understand what was happening, and the support of someone who knew how to navigate the American political system was essential. Philippe interceded so that the company would rehire Cromwell under the condition that the Frenchman would keep him under control.

Mark Hanna, whose campaign had received a generous donation from Cromwell, would be advocating the bill before the Senate and happily accepted the offer from Philippe and Cromwell to help him prepare for the debate. The peculiar duo united forces in order to teach Hanna about the tremendous advantages that Panama had over Nicaragua and to help him arrange the materials he would use in his address.

Philippe updated the small booklet he had used in his presentations for the United States the previous year and provided other useful materials: "Senator, the key to persuading people to favor Panama is to list the technical advantages in terms that are easy to understand and to get them to see the risks associated with the Nicaraguan route," he'd confidently told Hanna.

Cromwell, on the other hand, had prepared a number of questions and answers regarding the Canal Company, which he represented, since he knew that many of the attacks from Morgan, the chief proponent for Nicaragua, would be directed at the company and the way in which the French had managed it.

One afternoon, just before the initiation of the "Battle of the Routes," as it had come to be known by the press, Hanna invited Philippe and Cromwell to his house to celebrate the end of the preparations. Toasting with punch, he said to them, "Gentlemen, I think the strength of the arguments we have prepared will, without a doubt, convince my colleagues in the Senate of the benefits of Panama being the chosen route... Thank you."

The materials that Philippe and Cromwell had arranged would be very effective when it came time to persuade Hanna's colleagues and furthermore, gain votes for the Colombian route. Hanna was particularly pleased with a giant map of Central America where each county was marked with black or red dots. The red dots represented active volcanoes and the black dots were inactive volcanoes. Nicaragua had several red and black dots. Panama had none.

Just then, a miracle occurred. Two weeks before the beginning of the debate in the Senate, on May 14, a telegram from New Orleans went around, announcing the eruption of the Momotombo Volcano in Nicaragua. At the beginning of that same month, the Mount Peleé Volcano on the island of Martinique resulted in the deaths of 30,000 people and destruction of the city of Saint Pierre in a matter of minutes; the event had terrified the American people and the danger of volcanoes was fresh in the senators' minds.

The volcanoes were a real threat and soon many people began to question if Nicaragua would be a suitable place for construction of the canal. In addition, some newspapers such as the *New York Sun* asked senators to consider the risk presented by Momotombo.

When everyone was convinced that the eruption of Momotombo would ensure a winning vote for the Panamanian route, Senator Morgan unexpectedly released copies of a telegram from President Zelaya of Nicaragua to his ambassador in Washington, Mr. Corea: "The published reports regarding the recent volcanic activity in Nicaragua are completely false." The opportunity presented by Momotombo's eruption to eliminate support for Nicaragua had been eradicated by a cablegram of dubious origin.

25

June 1902

Senator Morgan was the first to speak: "The Panamanian problem has already been studied several times. Bancroft discussed it in his book, 'History of Central America.' The only way to stabilize Panama is to provide a strong external government. If the United States decides to build the canal in Panama, it will have to take Panama by force and I for one don't want to be part of that fight."

Senator Mitchell of Oregon was a bit more aggressive: "Panama is a sewer that we can't touch without contracting, with certainty, a deadly moral infection. It is a mountain of criminal excrement that not even all the water in the oceans could ever clean."

From the gallery intended for the public, Philippe observed with concern that the attack on the Panamanian route began with surprising aggression and that the majority of the Senate was in favor of Nicaragua.

The next day, it was Hanna's turn to speak. The senator, limping and followed by an aide who carried several books and documents, entered the senate floor that looked very different than it had just the day before: in the early morning hours, Philippe and Cromwell had put up numerous large maps which would serve as visual aides to their presentation.

Old, overweight, and sick, Mark Hanna spoke with difficulty but with certain conviction. Slowly but surely, he made his point that Panama was the best route for the canal: "We have passed the period of sentimentalism, Mr. President. We've passed the period of sentimentalism and the American people demand the canal be built on the ideal route. I understand that my colleagues have invested a great deal of time in researching the Nicaraguan route and that, naturally, they have a great predilection toward it, but the American people want us to choose the superior route, not the one we like best."

Mark Hanna took several days to present all the information Cromwell and Philippe and prepared: "The Panama Canal is 216 kilometers shorter than the Nicaraguan route; it will have less curves which will make the navigation of ships easier; it will allow crossing the isthmus in half the time that it would take in Nicaragua; it requires fewer locks; it has access to the intercontinental railway that we ourselves built five decades ago and which will be cheaper to finish and operate..."

Hanna's brilliant presentation, in addition to his credibility—he was rumored to be a potential presidential candidate due to certain powerful sectors being discontented with President Roosevelt—assured that many senators would be convinced to vote for the Panamanian route.

But Philippe didn't want to take any risks. Even though the technical reasons favored Panama, it was necessary to eliminate the sentimentality connected to Nicaragua. "Emotions are stronger than reason," he reminded Cromwell one afternoon over lunch in a nearby restaurant. In some way, he had to generate fear or mistrust in regard to Nicaragua. But the only thing that occurred to him was to rely on the volcanoes, which had been minimized by the supposed cablegram from President Zelaya. How does one expunge a president's claim that there hasn't been any recent volcanic activity?

One afternoon while walking from the Capitol to the New Willard Hotel, Philippe got to thinking how he would do it. All of a sudden, he remembered the letter sent by his former colleague, H.B. Slaven from Nicaragua, and the engineer ran to a stamp dealer not far from his hotel.

And there he found them: Nicaraguan stamps showing the majestic Momotombo in full eruption. An ecstatic Philippe bought ninety, one for each senator, brought them to the hotel, and with the help of the New Willard staff secretary, stuck them on individual sheets of paper and typed beneath each stamp: "An official witness of the volcanic activity on the Isthmus of Nicaragua."

On the morning of June 16, each senator found in his office an envelope containing the stamp sent by Philippe. This turned out to be the most effective weapon against Nicaragua. During one session, shortly before the debate had finished, Senator Gallinger asked if it were prudent to build the canal in a country that had so many volcanoes that they put them on their stamps.

Finally, Senator Spooner, another of Cromwell's allies, introduced a bill to formally elect Panama as the location where the United States would build the canal. In the vote for the Spooner Bill, Panama won in the Senate, 42 votes compared to 34 for Nicaragua, and later it would win with 259 votes to 8 in the House of Representatives.

POSTAGE STAMP OF THE REPUBLIC OF NICARAGUA.

An official witness of the volcanic activity on the Isthmus of Nicaragua.

Owing to an earthquake following an eruption of the volcano (to be seen smoking in the background) the wharf and the locomotive (to be seen in the foreground) were thrown into the lake with a large quantity of sacks of coffee, on the 24th of March, 1902, at 1.55 P. M. (*Iris de la Tarde* of Granada, and *Democracia* of Managua, two Nicaraguan papers. See also *New York Sun* of 12th of June, 1902.)

Note sent by Philippe Bunau-Varilla to U.S. Senators in order to convince them to select the Panama route instead of the Nicaraguan route. Courtesy of Weil Art Gallery, Panama.
Research at Library of Congress done by Neal West in 1991

26

Washington D.C., June 28, 1902

Philippe sat down on his hotel bed at the New Willard Hotel and began taking off his tie. He was tired after a day filled with emotion and he wanted to fall asleep as soon as possible. The following morning he would begin making preparations to see his children, who he'd spent very little time with in recent years.

That morning, President Roosevelt had signed the Spooner Act, which authorized him to buy all shares of the Panama Canal Company as well as the concession that the enterprise had with Colombia for no more than forty million dollars; and if he did not succeed, he would have to return to the Nicaraguan route and build the canal there.

The success of the day assured that soon Philippe would have time for other things unrelated to the canal: he would take a vacation and fulfill promises he'd made, especially the one he'd made to Etienne to see the *Aerodroma*, the flying machine being built by Samuel Langley. His son, who was staying in Bigelow's home in Manhattan, along with his mother and sister, had read a report about tests the inventor was going to conduct on the Potomac River and ever since, every time he spoke to his father, Etienne reminded him of the promise he'd made.

Seated with his hands on his knees, Philippe recalled some of the events that had led him to this moment. He remembered when at only 26 years old, he had become general director of the project in

Panama. He shivered as he recalled the yellow fever that had spared him, but not some of his colleagues; the tragedy suffered by Ferdinand de Lesseps; his success in lobbying North American politicians, and of the fortune he'd invested along the way.

Today, finally, after so many sacrifices, the French route had come out on top and the United States would have to construct their canal there. "Well, they should build the canal there," Philippe thought as he tried to relieve the tension in his neck by circling his head. There was still plenty of work to be done before he could claim victory, and without a doubt, several things could still go wrong. But for the first time, the wind was blowing in his direction: now he had the American government's word. "Old Morgan and his minions never imagined this would happen," he thought, satisfied.

As he began unbuttoning his shirt, someone knocked on the door. Philippe was exhausted and didn't want to get up: "Who is it?" he called from his bed. There was no response, but a few seconds later the person knocked again, this time much more vehemently.

It seemed strange that someone would be looking for him at this hour without the hotel reception calling ahead; maybe it was an emergency. He began walking toward the door and the knocking started again: "I'm coming, I'm coming!" He opened the door and saw a vaguely familiar man. His face was haggard and his eyes, teary, "Take it, take it, take it!"

The first punch was in the nose, the second sent him falling to the floor, and the third, a kick, broke a rib. "Goddamned French son of a bitch. The canal was ours, the canal was ours and you stole it! You stole it!"

Philippe recognized the man as the Nicaraguan ambassador, Gabriel Corea, before the man walked back down the hall and before sticky green saliva clouded his vision.

27

The White House, September 28, 1902

Theodore Roosevelt was furious, "I've had it with those despicable jackrabbits! Do they just not know how to behave? Do they think our army is always at their disposal?" His advisors had interrupted his afternoon tennis game with Ambassador Jules Jusserand, who had prudently excused himself to look at the gardens, which had recently been renovated by Mrs. Roosevelt.

Once again, the Panamanians were rebelling against Bogotá. And just like on several other occasions, the Colombian president asked the United States to help restore order. To several of Roosevelt's advisors, the gall of Morroquín was too much. Once again he was asking for help to eliminate the revolutionary movement in Panama, but he hadn't demonstrated an honest intent to have both nations sign a treaty that would allow the United States to complete the French canal in the Northern province.

"And this Marroquín, what is he thinking?" roared the President of the United States, red-faced and with his teeth peeking out from under his recently trimmed mustache. Motioning with his tennis racket, Roosevelt almost accidentally whacked John Hay, who avoided being hit on the head by awkwardly bending. The French ambassador, dressed in white just like his host, did his best to pass unnoticed among the roses.

What really bothered Roosevelt was that Colombia had once again changed their requirements to sign a treaty with the United States. Unexpectedly, they had raised the cost from seven to ten million dollars to transfer the French concession to the Americans, and aspired to concede only ten kilometers across the isthmus rather than the requested ten miles.

"President Roosevelt, Colombia is obliged to let us build the canal in Panama. The Treaty of 1846 with Colombia clearly states that our country has free reign to travel the isthmus by means of transport that now exist or will be constructed in the future. The building of the canal is implicit in the treaty that we already have with Colombia!" exclaimed Professor John Bassett Moore, as calmly as possible.

Alfred Thayer Mahan, another advisor who knew Panama very well after having been stationed there in the past, suggested to threaten Colombia with taking Panama by force if they didn't allow construction of the canal, since they were disregarding an existing international treaty that the United States had always honored.

"No, we have the elections coming up…" Roosevelt said.

John Hay intervened, "Mr. President, we could forget about Panama and take up negotiations with Nicaragua again. It's a simple and easy solution to the problem presented by Colombia. And it's in accordance with the Spooner Act."

The president lowered his gaze, wiped a piece of the lawn from his leather shoes with his racket and thought for a few seconds. "All right! Let's help those dagos control their rebels, but we will demand that they sign the treaty immediately."

And so the United States intervened once again to re-establish order in Panama and to protect the sovereign Colombia. A few weeks later, the Treaty of Peace was signed by liberals and conservatives on board the American gunboat *Wisconsin* at the port of Panama City.

Theodore Roosevelt Collection, Harvard College Library

Photo of Theodore Roosevelt.
Photo courtesy of the "Theodore Roosevelt Collection," from the
University of Harvard Library
(Roosevelt R500.P69a-089)

28

June 13, 1903

Almost a year had passed since President Roosevelt signed the Spooner Act and Bogotá still had given no clear sign of wanting to allow the United States to build the Panama Canal. Negotiations of the treaty between Dr. Tomás Herrán and John Hay had been quite challenging due to their uncompromising attitudes and the constantly changing conditions that the Colombians wanted to impose. Furthermore, all of this caused considerable distress in President Roosevelt which only added to the ordeal.

Philippe had to postpone his return home for Christmas because he had to mediate the negotiations, and fortunately, both sides were able to reach an agreement to sign what would become the Herrán-Hay Treaty. Smoking a Cuban on the first class deck of the steamship *Emideo* headed to *Le Havre*, Philippe celebrated Christmas Eve alone in the middle of the Atlantic.

Upon his arrival in Paris, just before the end of the year, Philippe received a pleasant surprise: his friend Francis Loomis had been named Assistant Secretary of State and would be working for John Milton Hay as of January 1903. Undeniably, the influence of Mr. Bigelow was second to none.

But for several months, the Colombian senate didn't seem to want to sign the treaty their country's ambassador had already endorsed. Even worse, rumors were circulating that the German ambassador in Bogotá was heavily lobbying for Colombia to reject the Herrán-Hay Treaty.

It was no secret that the Kaiser wanted to establish a strong presence in Latin America, even though this disregarded the Monroe Doctrine of an "America for Americans." It wasn't long before

President Roosevelt had to prevent the Kaiser from settling a debt owed to Germany by carrying out a "temporary occupation" of Venezuela.

According to what the American Ambassador in Colombia, Beaupré, told Loomis, the Germans wanted Bogotá to extend a new concession to them once the French concession expired in eighteen months, and then Germany would finish construction of the canal initiated by the French.

The Kaiser had even sent a team of engineers to inspect the Panamanian route. "Damned Prussians, hoping once again to tarnish the reputation of the French," Philippe said to Maurice, who responded with a smile, "Brother, what the Kaiser really wants is to control access to the nitrate in Chile…" Philippe never understood why Maurice felt such an affinity for the Germans.

In the face of Colombian indecision and then German threat, the engineer decided to send a lengthy cablegram to President Marroquín of Colombia, which said, among other things:

"Colombian failure to ratify the treaty would leave only two options: either the construction of the Nicaraguan Canal and consequently, the loss to Colombia of incalculable benefits resulting from construction of a great artery of universal commerce in Colombian territory, or construction of the Panama Canal after the secession and declaration of independence of the Panamanian isthmus, under the protection of the United States, equal to what has happened in Cuba."

It wasn't the first time that Philippe sent a message in which he openly mentioned the possibility of Panama becoming independent of Colombia. The past November, he had sent a similar cablegram, but hadn't received any response. Philippe couldn't explain how the Colombian President dared to ignore him.

Almost simultaneously, William Nelson Cromwell had arranged a secret meeting with President Roosevelt. As he left the White House, Cromwell gave instructions to his assistants and on the 13th of June, the *New York World* published a report titled: "The State of Panama is Ready to Become Independent if the Treaty is Rejected by the Colombian Congress."

The body of the article stated, among other things, the following: "It has been said that Roosevelt supports the idea…the United States will immediately recognize the new government in order to negotiate and sign the canal treaty." Almost instantaneously, other newspapers published similar reports.

And the White House remained silent.

29

September 1903

"Your presence is urgently needed. Look for Lindo in New York. Risk of losing everything. WNC." This was the text of the cablegram that Cromwell sent to Philippe in the beginning of September. Something terribly serious had to have happened for the lawyer to ask him to come to the United States.

Immediately, Philippe asked Ida to prepare little Giselle because they would all be going to the United States. Etienne, who was now thirteen years old, had gone to New York a few weeks earlier to visit the Bigelow's, where the rest of the family had planned to eventually join him; now however, they would be doing so sooner than later.

All of them except for Philippe. His family could enjoy the Bigelow's kindness but he had to take care of the canal; the threat that the United States could revisit the Nicaraguan route and forget about Panama had returned after the Colombian Senate's rejection of the Herrán-Hay Treaty.

"Damned Prussians! They've managed to sabotage the ratification of the treaty..." Philippe told an uninterested Maurice.

Two days after hearing about the Colombian "no," President Roosevelt had lunched with Senator Shelby Cullom at *Sagamore Hill*, his family home. Cullom had given an interview immediately after to several reporters: "Senator Cullom, how will the canal be built without a treaty with Colombia? Are we going back to Nicaragua?"

Cullom, without hesitation responded, "We'll simply sign another treaty, not with Colombia, but with Panama."

Arriving in New York, Philippe sent his wife and daughter to the Bigelow's house and then immediately went to find Joshua Lindo at his office. Lindo, head of one of the most well-established banks in

Panama, usually did business with the Canal Company, and consequently, knew Cromwell and the other most prominent men on the isthmus quite well. Though Philippe had known the banker for several years, it had been a long time since they'd seen one another.

"Philippe, welcome. Please, come into my office." Lindo's face foretold bad news. As he entered, Philippe saw a haggard Cromwell slumped in a chair. He was pale and his hair and mustache were disheveled. He looked like he hadn't bathed or changed his clothes for days.

Lindo spoke first: "We have a grave problem. Cromwell brought Gabriel Duque, the Panamanian businessman, to meet with Secretary Hay to discuss the plan and Duque betrayed us. After confirming that the United States supported the plan, Duque went directly to Ambassador Herrán and told him everything. Herrán already informed Bogotá and made a formal complaint to Secretary Hay."

Philippe was furious: "You went with Duque to John Hay's office and didn't tell me? I thought we had a gentlemen's agreement to keep each other informed and work together on all of this! Why did you do it?" Cromwell avoided Philippe's fiery blue eyes and didn't answer.

"Please Philippe, this isn't the time to place blame ..." Lindo said.

"Of course I blame Mr. Cromwell! We have worked together for a long time and I have always honored our agreement. What else have you done without telling me? How could you do something so shameless as bringing a revolutionary to the Secretary of State? And why Duque? What happened with Amador?"

Cromwell sat in silence, beaten. Philippe, beside himself, lunged at the lawyer but Lindo intervened.

"Philippe, please! What's done is done. Now we have to solve the problem. Ambassador Herrán is threatening to cancel the concession if it's proven that the Canal Company," he said, gesturing toward the lawyer, "is promoting the sedition of Panama."

Philippe couldn't believe that Cromwell would have risked everything, probably to appear and be known as the plan's creator. Lindo continued, "Cromwell will soon be leaving the United States; it's best that he's as far from Washington as possible. But we need you to meet with Amador."

***

Philippe was in his usual room at the Waldorf Astoria Hotel when there was a knock at the door. This time he knew who it was: Dr. Manuel Amador Guerrero, his long-time acquaintance from Panama who had worked beneath him when Philippe assumed general command of the project several years ago. After an affectionate greeting, Philippe asked, "Tell me, Dr. Amador, what can I do for you?" Lindo thought it best that Amador didn't know that the engineer had worked with Cromwell, and Philippe pretended not to know a thing.

In spite of all the years that had passed, the elderly doctor had retained the vitality and sharp thinking that Philippe had remembered so well. Amador was a true Panamanian patriot, who had dedicated his life to improving the quality of life for his countrymen.

The doctor said that various prominent Panamanians, many of whom Philippe knew very well, were organizing to bring about a revolution. They had already secured the help of Colombian soldiers stationed in Panama, since after years of being there they considered themselves locals. Furthermore, Bogota had failed to pay them for many months and General Huertas agreed to support the secession if he and his men were monetarily awarded.

But this time, they wanted the support of the United States in initiating the revolt. Since everyone knew that Cromwell, the lawyer for the Canal Company and the Railway, had excellent political connections, he was asked to help, and he promised to do so. But for some reason unknown to Amador, soon the Colombians soon knew about his plans, and Cromwell was avoiding him at all cost.

"If something happens to my colleagues because of that lawyer, I'll kill him myself!" Amador exclaimed as he mimicked strangulation with his hands. Philippe could barely hold back a smile as he thought, "I'll gladly help."

When the doctor finished explaining his plan, Philippe got up from his chair and, in a disapproving tone, said: "Dr. Amador, I'm terribly sorry for what's happening, but you are responsible for having trusted something so important to inexperienced people. However, I might be able to help you."

You want six million dollars to buy gunboats and weapons. It's too much money and perhaps, unnecessary. Stay in New York and

I'll call you soon. As we should both be discreet, if you call by telephone, identify yourself as 'Smith.' I will use the name 'Jones' to contact you."

When Dr. Amador Guerreo went to the Hotel Endicott to wait, Philippe called his friend at the Department of State.

Portrait of Dr. Manuel Amador Guerrero.
Photo taken from the book "Panamá, la creación, destrucción y resurrección"
by Philippe Bunau-Varilla

30

The moment Etienne had been long-awaiting was finally here, and for the first time since he could remember, his father hadn't let him down. Seated along the Potomac River among a small group of spectators, they waited anxiously for the *Aerodroma* to make its first flight.

It was an unusually cool morning, but Philippe and Etienne were bundled up and waited eagerly to see the flying machine developed by Professor Samuel F. Langley, secretary of the Smithsonian Institute. The Department of War was sponsoring the project and the day's test launch had generated grand excitement, not only for the general public, but for the United States government.

A large raft, 26 meters long by three meters wide, with a workshop on its platform, would serve as the base from which the *Aerodroma* would launch. On the workshop's roof, manual cranes to raise the apparatus and place it onto launch rails were incorporated into a structure that indicated that the machine was ready to fly. The cabin was lined with blankets to hide the 28 horsepower gasoline engine which would propel the take-off.

At twelve o'clock sharp, the man in charge of operating *Aerodroma*, Professor Manley, dressed in his aeronautical suit, climbed into the cabin and began testing the engine. The crowd went wild upon hearing the wondrous machine start up, proving itself. The four wings, seven meters each, along with the propellers looked like something out of a Jules Verne book.

"Thank you, papa," said an excited Etienne, squeezing his father's hand. The excitement of the crowd and the revolutionary nature of the sight inevitably reminded Philippe of the Panama Canal:

the difficulty, the impossibility of a grand idea that would finally be validated for the world to see. Today, Langley would demonstrate that a machine could fly. Soon Philippe would complete the construction of the Panama Canal, in honor of France.

At twelve fifteen, exactly on time, the announcer requested the crowd's silence so that Professor Manley could concentrate on the takeoff. An assistant appeared at the end of the twenty-two meter rails and signaled to Manley. The motor started and gradually increased in power until it died...

Almost immediately, the pilot restarted and revved the engine until two assistants removed the chocks that kept the machine from taking off.

Unfortunately, the flight lasted only an instant: the *Aerodroma* fell into the river and a soaking Professor Manley had to be helped out of the icy waters.

"Panama is different," Philippe thought as he got up to take Etienne back to the hotel where he and Giselle were staying with their mother. The elder Bunau-Varilla had to prepare what he would say to the president when they met. Francis Loomis had arranged for Philippe to meet with Roosevelt in the coming days and if he managed to secure support for his plan, although indirect support, everything would go well.

Previous page: Photo of Dr. Langley's *Aerodroma* before its test flight.
Photo: United States Library of Congress

Photo of Dr. Langley's *Aerodroma* as it attempts flight.
Photo: United States Library of Congress

31

Washington D.C., October 9. 1903

The carriage stopped at 1600 Pennsylvania Avenue. Careful not to dishevel his clothing, Philippe stepped down and walked toward the main entrance of the executive mansion. He presented his identification to the guard and then a member of the recently created Secret Service escorted him inside. From there, they climbed the stairway to where Loomis was waiting for them on the second floor landing.

"Thank you, I'll take care of Mr. Bunau-Varilla from here. Good day, Philippe. Please follow me; the president is expecting us," his friend said, signaling toward the presidential office door on the other side of the corridor. Another Secret Service member, an enormous man with broad jaws and who looked like a boxer, held his post outside the president's office. As he walked toward the door separating him from Roosevelt, Philippe noticed an archway to his right that lead to a hallway where two children were playing with a strange toy. Unable to resist temptation, Philippe said, "Hello children, what is that thing?"

"It's an electric express," Archibald Roosevelt said, "Mr. Lionel gave it to us. Big Bill loves it, right Bill?" Blushing, the bodyguard at the president's door smiled and nodded.

"Without a doubt, it's the most wonderful toy I've ever seen…" Philippe said, genuinely excited. The other boy, Quentin, ran toward Philippe, "And this is Daddy!" he exclaimed, showing Philippe a stuffed bear.

"Archibald, Quentin! Let the gentlemen pass by!" Edith Roosevelt said, from a rocking chair obscured by the wall of the archway. Realizing that he was in the presence of the First Lady,

Philippe approached the entrance to the hallway and bowed as if he were greeting royalty. "Mrs. Roosevelt, my name is Philippe Bunau-Varilla, it's a pleasure to meet you."

"Good afternoon, Mr. Bunau-Varilla, pleased to meet you. Good afternoon to you too, Mr. Loomis. I think Teddy is waiting for you." She smiled and returned to her reading.

The office door was now open and William "Big Bill" Craig, his gray eyes observing Philippe closely, followed them inside and closed the door behind them.

Theodore Roosevelt was standing behind his desk when they entered, in the midst of reviewing a stack of documents. A rosebud that his wife had collected from the garden that morning adorned his lapel. His smile revealed his large teeth beneath his mustache. "Mr. Bunau-Varilla, dee-lighted!" Roosevelt said, walking around his large walnut desk to shake Philippe's hand.

This engineer had something different from the other visitors Roosevelt had received in his office. Normally, a person coming to see him for the first time was anxious and timid. However, the small Frenchman seemed to look at Roosevelt as though he was measuring him up for a duel. "Mr. President, thank you for having us in the Executive Mansion..."

"White House," Roosevelt corrected, smiling as he firmly shook Philippe's hand. "Mr. Loomis tells me that you own the newspaper, *Le Matin*. How is the world of journalism, Mr. Bunau-Varilla?"

Loomis intervened to mention that *Le Matin* had helped to clear up the famous case of Captain Alfred Dreyfus, Phillipe's old friend from the Polytechnic School who had been wrongly accused of leaking French military secrets to Germany.

Philippe recognized his cue, "Mr. President, Captain Dreyfus isn't the only victim of detestable political passions. Panama is another."

"Ah yes, you have dedicated plenty of time and effort to Panama, Mr. Bunau-Varilla. Well, what do you think will be the resolution for the present situation?" Roosevelt asked to Philippe's relief, since he had feared that the president wouldn't want to discuss the topic.

Making the most of his opportunity, Philippe responded boldly, "Mr. President, a revolution!"

Roosevelt feigned surprise, "A revolution... What makes you

think that's the answer?"

"Several factors, Mr. President." Philippe hesitated for a second but decided to capitalize this anticipated meeting to ask the question he had rehearsed in his head, "If you'll allow me to ask you something, Mr. President, do you think the United States would support an armed revolution in Panama?"

Loomis got up from his seat, visibly upset by the audacity of his friend. Roosevelt didn't answer.

"Would the U.S. protect Colombia instead?" Philippe insisted, to the further astonishment of Loomis.

"I can only say that I don't have any sympathy for a government that behaves the way that they have." Roosevelt got up to extend his hand to his visitor, "Mr. Bunau-Varilla, it's been a pleasure to have you but I have other things to attend to."

William Craig opened the door to the office and accompanied Philippe to the first floor foyer. There, frustrated at not managing to secure the unequivocal support of the president, he waited for Loomis to come down. His friend was undoubtedly furious at him, but Philippe didn't regret using his opportunity to ask Roosevelt directly if his country would support a revolt in Panama. The president's eyes and tone, Philippe believed, had betrayed him.

A few minutes later, Francis Loomis walked toward Philippe, who got up to explain why he had been so direct, but Loomis' smile told him it would be better to just listen. "Relax, Philippe," Loomis said in a soothing voice, "I have a gift for you from Secretary Hay, who is sick and apologizes for not having been able to attend our meeting with the president. He says he is sure you will enjoy your present if you pay attention."

***

That afternoon, Philippe took the train to New York. Seated in first class, he was still replaying in his mind the conversation he'd had with the president when he remembered the book that Loomis had given him at the executive mansion.

"Let's see if Secretary Hay and I share the same literary tastes," he thought sarcastically.

The book was titled *Captain Macklin*. Philippe immediately recognized the author, Richard Harding Davis, whose stories were very popular in the United States. Advertisements for his novels were often in New York and Washington newspapers, but Philippe had never read any of them.

As he examined the text, he found a blank piece of paper marking page 74. In the last paragraph of this page, a dot had been penciled next to a statement made by Aiken, one of the characters:

You should understand that the Central American Republics are under the thumb of a large enterprise, bank or railway. For example, all of these revolutions you read about in the papers very seldom find their support among the people. The people do not choose presidents. That is the work of some enterprise in New York that wants a concession...

Philippe couldn't believe what he was reading. Speechless, he placed the book to the side and looked away, his eyes penetrating the darkness punctuated by railway lights passing by as the train moved onward to New York. He thought for a few moments and then returned to the book. Just as he was about to turn the page, a waiter came to offer him something to drink.

"No!" Philippe spat.

He continued reading Aikin's dialogue on the page where he'd opened the book: *If the country's president doesn't give the concession, the company will begin to look to one who will. It will meet with a political rival or an army general who wants to be president, and they all want that, and come to an agreement with him. They will promise that if he starts a revolution, the company will supply him with money and weapons. Of course, the agreement is that if the leader of the revolution is successful, he will give the patrons in New York whatever they want. Sometimes they want a concession for a railway, sometimes it's a nitrate mine or a rubber forest, but you can bet that there are very few revolutions that aren't supported by a business agreement.*

Philippe closed the book, placed it aside, and then immediately opened it again to the beginning. There he found another surprise: the prologue was written by none other than Theodore Roosevelt! Davis had fought in the Cuban war as part of Roosevelt's regiment and since then they had maintained a strong friendship.

From that moment on, Philippe didn't stop reading except to get off the train and check into his room at the Waldorf Astoria. There, he continued to devour the tome with a mix of surprise and excitement. According to the story, French General Laguerre formed an alliance with Royal Macklin, the novel's main character, to incite a revolution in Honduras.

There was no question. Even though the declaration couldn't be made openly, the American government was confirming to Philippe that they would support a revolution in Panama.

New York Tribune, book ads.
December 05, 1902. This Chapter contains excerpts from the public domain novel, Royal Macklin, by Richard Harding Davis.
Image Source: Library of Congress

32

October 13, 1903

A few days had passed since his visit to the White House and Philippe already had his plan ready to bring about a Panamanian revolution. Now he only needed to convince Dr. Amador to execute the plan.

Philippe went down to the lobby at the Waldorf Astoria and made two phone calls. The first call was to his lawyer, Frank Pavey, to ask for a copy of the Cuban Constitution. Then he called Dr. Amador and invited him to the hotel as soon as possible.

When Amador arrived, Philippe had a map of the isthmus pinned to the wall of his room and immediately began explaining his plan: Amador and his men would begin the revolt in Panama City so that when Colombia sent their troops from Cartagena, as they usually did, they would have to disembark in Colón to then cross the isthmus by train, which was controlled by supporters of the revolution. At the right time, the movement would extend to Colón and when the rebels had taken over both cities, Amador and his men would declare independence from Colombia.

Meanwhile, Philippe would ensure that the United States facilitated the revolution using the same treaty that had protected the sovereignty of Colombia in the past. Once Amador had control of both coasts and declared independence, Philippe would be responsible for making sure the Americans rapidly recognized the Republic of Panama and extended their protection.

It would no longer be necessary to buy gunboats or much weaponry. Philippe would use one hundred thousand dollars of his personal fortune to pay the soldiers' salaries and to give Huertas a bonus, but only in exchange for the new government naming him

Minister Extraordinary and Plenipotentiary to the United States. Once the new canal treaty was signed, the new nation would receive the ten million dollars originally meant for Colombia. "And the Canal Company would receive the corresponding forty million," he added casually.

Amador was astonished: "Philippe, assuming you are able to do what you say, your plan seems fine. But there is no chance of us naming you minister to the United States. You aren't even Panamanian and it's been almost twenty years since you've visited the isthmus! How do you know what is best for us?"

"This is my only offer, Dr. Amador. Furthermore, how do you expect me to gain recognition for the new republic if I'm not your minister to the United States?" Philippe asked innocently.

Amador was so upset with his former boss he almost didn't even say goodbye. "Mr. Bunau-Varilla, you are asking me for something I cannot and will not grant you."

As he opened the door for his guest, the Frenchman said, "You can accept my offer or try to get your friend Cromwell to continue to support you. Think about it, Dr. Amador."

The following morning someone knocked on the door to room 1162. It was Amador, looking exhausted after a sleepless night. "Fine, Philippe. Let's do it."

Immediately, the French engineer began working with Frank Pavey to draft a Declaration of Independence. He also wrote a constitution for Panama using the Cuban Constitution for reference and created a secret code to communicate through cablegrams. When he finally decided to join his family at the Bigelow's summer house in Highland Falls, he first made a stop at Macy's in Manhattan.

Walking through the wide aisles full of clothing, perfume, hats and the largest selection of goods imaginable, Philippe, who never went to this type of establishment, finally got to the fabric department. "Good morning, ma'am. I need to buy red, yellow, and blue fabric."

The young salesclerk responded, "With pleasure, sir. What type of fabric are you looking for?"

"What material is normally used to make flags?" asked the small Frenchman with the giant mustache, obviously excited.

"Silk Department at Macy´s, circa late 1880´s. Courtesy Of Macy's Inc. Archives"

33

New York

Even though Amador had yet to leave for Panama to carry out his plan, Philippe needed a diplomatic uniform for when he went to introduce his credentials as Minister Plenipotentiary to President Roosevelt.

A sober and elegant diplomatic uniform, but congruent with the fledgling country he was going to represent, that was what he needed. The problem was that because the American government had prohibited the use of unauthorized diplomatic uniforms for several decades, the tailors specialized in the art of fashioning such garments were scarce.

In the European diplomatic world, the United States custom of sending poorly dressed officials to important events was quite famous. The most memorable case was that of Benjamin Franklin, who appeared before the French court in a simple suit that was poorly altered to look like a diplomatic uniform. This would not be the case for Philippe.

When he went to present his credentials, he would do it in elegant dress appropriate for the occasion. Although he had wanted to have the uniform tailored at Hawkes & Company in London, there wasn't enough time.

One night, while conversing with Baron Komura of Japan over supper at the Waldorf restaurant, Komura commented, "Actually, the solution is quite simple, Mr. Bunau-Varilla. Just look for the best tailor of military uniforms and he will undoubtedly be able to fashion you something appropriate for the diplomatic world."

At first, Philippe had assumed that because Baron Komura had studied at Harvard, he would know President Roosevelt quite well, and therefore, Philippe hoped to gain the Baron's trust. However, Roosevelt and Komura had studied in separate programs so Philippe's assumption was untrue. Still, since Komura also spent a great deal of time at the Waldorf, they soon established a cordial relationship and learned they had plenty in common. Like Philippe, Komura came from a working class family and had been able to study at an elite university thanks to a scholarship.

"I know that Count Cassini once went to a military tailor at 65 Fifth Avenue and he was very pleased with the resulting diplomatic uniform," Komura stated. This caught Philippe's attention: if Count Cassini had had a diplomatic uniform tailored by this man, he must be very good.

The next morning, Philippe went to visit Joseph F. Webber, a military tailor with an excellent reputation for using the finest materials and for producing garments of supreme quality. A few days later, when Philippe tried on his uniform for the first time, he was delighted with the gold trim Webber had incorporated into the collar and cuffs. Looking at himself in the mirror as the tailor tested the uniform for fit, Philippe smiled as he thought he was going to need a medal to complete his look.

The cover of this book shows Philippe Bunau-Varilla dressed in his diplomatic uniform.

34

October 20, 1903

Before the elderly doctor boarded the steamship *Yucatán*, which would sail directly to Panama, Philippe reminded Amador, "Remember, doctor, if you don't send me a telegram affirming that I will be named Minister Plenipotentiary, in accordance with our agreement, I can't be responsible for what happens."

Amador had with him all of the documents Philippe had given him, plus a flag similar to that of the United States, except instead of white it had yellow, and the stars had been substituted by two suns united by a canal. "Isn't it beautiful? My wife made it with the help of Mrs. Bigelow last Sunday..." Philippe said, obviously proud of how well his design had come out. Amador didn't respond.

It took an agonizing week for the *Yucatán* to get to Panama. To reduce his anxiety, brought on by the wait, Philippe devoted himself to taking care of any formalities with his bank to make sure the hundred thousand dollars he had promised to the rebels would be available. On the 27th of October, when Amador had arrived, Philippe waited to receive a message from his accomplice. But no form of communication came through.

Two more days passed before Philippe finally received a coded message:

DESTINATION BAD NEWS POWERFUL TIGER. URGE VAPOR COLON . –SMITH

Using the previously agreed upon code, Philippe translated the message:

"This message is for Bunau-Varilla. Colombian troops arrive from the Atlantic. Five days. More than 200. Message sent by Amador." The rest, "urge vapor Colon," was written in Spanish, not in code, and meant that the rebels were asking Philippe to send an American gunboat as soon as possible.

Philippe didn't believe that the Colombian troops were actually going to Colón, but rather, that Amador and his men wanted to see if the Frenchman would follow through with his offer to mobilize the American Army, which seemed reasonable after Cromwell's unfortunate intervention.

Immediately, Philippe took a train to Washington to visit Francis Loomis. When he got to his friend's office, he got right to the point, "Francis, it is of crucial importance that by the 3rd of November the United States has a gunboat guarding the port of Colón. We don't want a repeat of the events of 1885 when Prestán rebelled and the entire city burned up because the United States didn't intervene in time to maintain order. The canal needs a gunboat to go to Colón as soon as possible."

Loomis looked squarely at Philippe and responded with utmost sincerity, "It would be a shame to repeat those events. This time we will be prepared. Look, I want you to talk to the Secretary of State Hay. It's time you two met." That night, Philippe sent a cablegram to Amador confirming in coded text that the gunboat was set to arrive in two and a half days.

On November 2nd, at the end of the day, the gunboat *Nashville* anchored down in Colón. Philippe had demonstrated to the Panamanians that he was true to his word.

For Amador, who was discouraged by his comrades' rejection of Phillippe's plan, seeing *Nashville* at the port, proving the Frenchman's words, gave him renewed hope to follow the plan and put it into motion the following day.

35

November 3, 1903

That morning the Colombian troops arrived in Colón at the charge of General Juan Tovar, disembarked with no trouble, and immediately headed to the interoceanic train station where they were received by Colonel James Shaler, superintendent of the railway.

"General Tovar, welcome to Colón."

"Good morning Colonel Shaler. I need to take the train with all of my men to Panama City immediately," Tovar said in perfect English.

"I'm sorry, but we don't have enough space available right now. I suggest you take your officials with you in one of the available cars, and when we can, we'll send the rest of your soldiers to meet with you," Shaler smiled. "No thank you, I prefer to wait until we are all able to go together."

Shaler insisted, "General Tovar, Governor Obaldía specifically asked me to get you and your officials to Panama City immediately. He seems to urgently require your presence. The time of departure for the train has already passed and it doesn't make sense to have you all out here sitting under the sun. Please, board the train with your officials and I assure you that your soldiers will arrive soon."

In New York, Philippe was surprised to read a press release announcing the arrival and disembarkation of five hundred Colombian soldiers in Colón. Amador hadn't lied after all. Without a doubt, that many soldiers could thwart the revolutionaries' plans; if the plan failed now, several years would have to pass before a similar opportunity would present itself and for the first time, Philippe was genuinely afraid he wouldn't be able to complete the canal in Panama.

At the kindness of Shaler and the request of Governor Obaldía that they immediately move to the other coast, Tovar finally conceded to take the available train that was ready to go. Still doubtful about leaving all of his soldiers in Colón, the general watched as the image of Colonel Shaler, smiling and waving goodbye, became smaller and smaller.

When he arrived, Tovar was received with honor by General Esteban Huertas and various local dignitaries, as was custom, and finally, he was taken to the barracks that served as the Colombian military base in Panama. There, Tovar intended to inform Huertas that he was being relieved of his command, and that Tovar would be leading the Colombian military in Panama. However, once inside the barracks, Huertas spoke first, "General Tovar, you and your men are under arrest. Please hand over your sword."

When they heard about the arrest of Tovar and his vain attempt to resist, Amador and several supporters arrested Governor Obaldía, who was in favor of the revolution, but was also a representation of Colombian authority in Panama. That afternoon, the City Council declared independence and Amador, José Augustín Arango, Tomás Arias, Ricardo Arias, Federico Boyd, Carlos C. Arosemana, Manuel Espinoza Batista y Nicanor de Obarrio among others, were applauded by the crowd outside the Panama City Cathedral.

That night in New York, at Ida Bigelow's insistence, Philippe returned to the Bigelow's home for a dinner, entertainment, and relaxation after the nervous breakdown from which he'd been suffering since reading about the arrival of the Colombian troops in Panama. When he got back to his hotel, he found a cablegram from Amador that said: "Independence of the isthmus declared without bloodshed."

It was an excellent note and Philippe felt great relief in knowing that there was still hope. But things could still go wrong: Colón remained in Colombian hands.

American soldiers preparing arms in the streets of Colón.
Photo courtesy of the Authority of the Panama Canal.

The following days in Colón were filled with uncertainty as Colonel Eliseo Torres, who Tovar had left in charge of the soldiers, demanded the immediate release of his superiors. Tensions were raising so much that on several occasions Colombian and United States soldiers, who had arrived to maintain order according to the treaty with Colombia, were near the point of initiating a blood-filled confrontation.

Meanwhile in New York, Philippe had just finished reading a cablegram sent by Amador requesting the agreed upon money in order to pay the soldiers immediately. Even though his first instinct was to not send the money because Amador still hadn't confirmed that the Frenchman would be named Minister Plenipotentiary, Philippe asked banker, Joshua Lindo, to send 25,000 dollars to Panama. Clearly Amador needed to make some payments and it would be a mistake to send nothing at all.

The next day in Panama, Tovar, in his cell, received a visit from Dr. Amador.

"General Tovar, Panama is independent. We have the support of the United States and five thousand American soldiers are about to arrive to protect our new republic. I admire your position, but it won't get you anywhere. We are sending you back to Colón and from there you will return to Colombia."

"Absolutely not. We are going to protect Colombian sovereignty regardless of the consequences. Colonel Torres is very aware of his responsibilities and I know he is doing what he must."

Amador approached the bars separating him from General Tovar, "Torres and his soldiers are already aboard the steamship *Orinoco* and have begun the return to Cartagena. We've shown them our appreciation. Come on, the train is waiting to take you back to Colón."

After saying goodbye to Tovar, who still couldn't believe what Amador had told him, the doctor immediately went to send a message to Philippe:

"Today, this 6th of November, we will declare to the Secretary of State that Colón and all of the towns on the isthmus have adhered to the Declaration of Independence proclaimed in our capital. The authority of the Republic of Panama is being obeyed throughout the territory. Press the United States government to recognize the Republic of Panama."

Philippe knew, because of the press, that Colombia had threatened to send more troops to both Panamanian coasts and to eliminate this new intent to secede. The Revolutionary Junta couldn't risk losing support at this time when the recognition and protection of the United States was so urgent, so he responded to Amador:

"Ask the Junta to send me the message we agreed upon on the 20th of October, before you embark to Panama. This message will allow me to resolve urgent political and financial issues. This was our agreement. If I am not designated Minister Plenipotentiary to the United States, I will not intercede so that the Republic of Panama will be recognized. I reject all responsibility for what happens in the future if the Government of Panama prefers another solution. My hands will be tied, but my heart remains the same."

Two and a half hours after sending the message to Amador, Philippe received the following cablegram from Francisco de la Espriella, Minister of Exterior Relations:

"The Provisional Government Board of the Republic of Panama names the Recipient Minister Extraordinary and Plenipotentiary to the government of the United States of America with absolute power in political and financial negotiations."

That afternoon, Philippe celebrated with a bottle of champagne in the company of Joshua Lindo at the Waldorf Astoria restaurant.

36

"Today we are going to make history, Etienne," Philippe smiled as he fixed his son's tie in the lobby outside Secretary John Hay's office. He was pleased to finally be able to debut his elegant diplomatic uniform. In a few minutes, they would go to the White House to present Philippe's credentials to President Roosevelt, and to inform him that the new Republic of Panama would be formally recognized by the United States Government.

Philippe and Hay got into the official Secretary of State carriage and headed to the White House. Etienne followed in an elegant horse-drawn carriage that Philippe had rented especially for the occasion. Upon their arrival, they were quickly taken to the Blue Room where they were received by President Roosevelt and other officials. Hay formally introduced Philippe, who asked permission to give a short speech, previously edited by Hay:

"Mr. President, by allowing the Minister Plenipotentiary of the Republic of Panama to present to you his credentials, you are admitting the youngest and most fragile republic of the New World into the family of nations. This new republic was born into freedom from despotism that…"

Etienne wasn't paying attention to his father's discourse, nor was he paying attention to the exquisite decorations of the Blue Room. Everything was new, from the white paneling and the celestial paint on the walls, to the gigantic crystal candelabra hanging from the center of the room. The thirteen year-old was much more interested in the magnificent Bengal tiger hide next to a white piano, which, with its shining eyes and threatening fangs looked like he was about to leap at the guests at any second.

Roosevelt formally responded to Philippe:

"This government recognizes the right of the Panamanian inhabitants to declare their independence by way of a republic in form and spirit, just as we did almost a century ago when the people of Latin America proclaimed their right to popular government. Our wish for the people of Panama is that their new nation will enjoy stability and prosperity in harmony with the United States and that we will be able to open a new route for universal commerce. For you, Mr. Minister, my greatest wishes are that the mission entrusted to you will be successful."

With that, the ceremony was over and Roosevelt began to exit. But when Secretary Hay introduced Etienne, the president stopped to affectionately greet the young man.

"Mr. President, did you kill this tiger?" the young Bunau-Varilla asked, smiling nervously.

Forgetting his other responsibilities, the President of the United States knelt on the animal hide and for a half hour, told Etienne about his expedition to India. Amazed and terrified, the boy listened to how this tiger had devoured one of the guides during the night before Roosevelt managed to hunt him down.

As the president explained to Etienne the correct way to mount an elephant, Secretary Hay took Philippe aside, "Mr. Minister, what is this about a committee coming from Panama to negotiate the Canal Treaty? I thought we were signing with you. I read about it this morning in the newspaper and to be honest, I'm surprised you didn't mention something before."

Obviously bothered by the mention of Amador and his people, Philippe answered, "Mr. Secretary, I am just as surprised. You know how unpredictable the Colombians are; they always change agreements to their liking. Please remember that until recently, these Panamanians were Colombians and history could repeat itself... But since Amador and the others have not yet arrived, you can negotiate with me."

Hay immediately replied, "Mr. Minister, it will be a pleasure to sign with you. I will try to get it to you by Saturday morning."

The Blue Room at the White House, early 1900's.
Photo: United States Library of Congress

***

All Saturday, Philippe fought the temptation to go to Hay's house to retrieve the treaty. There was no time to lose; after all, the committee from Panama would be arriving in New York on Tuesday the 17th and if the agreement wasn't signed when they got there, everything was in danger. Knowing that he would need help with revision of the document, Philippe asked his lawyer, Frank Pavey, to come to New York.

Sunday morning, a messenger finally arrived at the New Willard Hotel to deliver the document. When he opened the envelope, Philippe discovered that the "new" pact was the same Herrán-Hay Treaty that had been rejected by Colombia. The only difference was the addition of some small suggestions that the Secretary of State had penciled in. "What a waste of time! Why did it take two days to send me this?" Philippe thought angrily.

After carefully looking over the document, he decided it was too risky to use the same contract that Colombia had already rejected. He had to draw up a new one that would be much more attractive to the United States and that the Senate would have no problem approving.

"Frank, we need to create a new treaty far more beneficial to the United States. It has to be attractive enough to surpass all possible opposition in Congress. We can't risk Morgan and his associates finding any reason to revisit the Nicaraguan route," Philippe said, and then went on to list the major changes that would have to be made to the contract.

The lawyer was taken aback, "But Philippe, shouldn't you consult with Amador and his men about these changes? You're making the treaty permanent, you are giving the United States sovereignty over the Panamanian territory!"

Visibly irritated, Philippe exploded, "Those reckless men think they are at the same level as the Secretary of State, they think they can negotiate like I have. No! I'm not going to let them ruin years of work with their inexperience. I won't allow them to toss me aside. I'll be the one to sign the treaty!"

Frank Pavey had never seen this aggressive side of his friend and client. "Philippe, with all due respect..."

"Mr. Pavey, I am paying you very well to do this job. If you can't do what I ask, I will find another lawyer who will. Can I count on you or not?"

***

On Wednesday the 18th, Philippe got up at four in the morning and went out to walk around the city. He hadn't been able to sleep that night, worried that if Hay put off revising the new treaty and the Panamanians arrived before he was able to sign it, all could be lost.

Philippe exited through the front entrance of the New Willard Hotel, turned to the right, and walked along Pennsylvania Avenue until he came to the fence surrounding the White House. "If only Roosevelt knew the precious time we are losing..." he thought while wishing he could knock on the door and inform the president that the Secretary's tedious attention to detail was putting the canal in danger. In a few hours the Panamanian delegation would arrive and take control of the negotiation if it wasn't already finished, resulting in Philippe being eliminated from the treaty's mediation.

He headed back toward 15th Street and walked south until he reached the Washington Monument, where he found a bench to sit down. He was too emotional at the moment.

He wanted to be with Mr. Bigelow who was the closest thing to a father Philippe had ever had, and in this moment he needed someone to guide and calm him. He was so nervous that suddenly, without realizing, he began to cry out of fear: fear of failure, fear that the canal would never be finished, fear of going home, fear of being the laughingstock to all those who had opposed the construction of the canal in Panama.

A short while later, a bit calmer and now hungry, Philippe began his return to the New Willard Hotel. When he got to the lobby, the first thing he did was go to the reception desk to see if he had received a message from Secretary Hay. Nothing. So he went to his room to bathe and change for breakfast with his lawyer at nine in the morning.

During breakfast, Philippe was so quiet that Pavey tried to cheer him up with a joke, "In all the years I've known you, you've never been quiet more than a minute. It's been a half hour and you haven't said a word. This is a milestone!" Philippe didn't smile but only looked at the piece of meat and potatoes his lawyer was eating.

The rest of the morning was torture. At lunchtime, Philippe didn't have an appetite so he stayed in his room waiting for the call that it was time to sign the treaty.

Meanwhile, lunch was just about over at John Hay's house, where various members of President Roosevelt's cabinet had dined. The host summed up the discussion with the following comments: "Gentlemen, I believe we can all agree that the new treaty is extremely advantageous for the United States and, let's be honest, not so much so for the Republic of Panama." When his guests finished laughing, he continued: "We must recognize that some of the clauses would be rejected by any Panamanian patriot. But if this is what we are offered, I think we ought to accept." And with that, the United States Government agreed with the treaty that Philippe had proposed.

The anxiously awaited envelope arrived at three in the afternoon. His hands trembling, Philippe opened it to discover an invitation to Secretary Hay's home at six o'clock that evening.

37

That night, Manuel Amador, Federico Boyd, and Carlos Arosemena would arrive in Washington from New York. The newspapers announced that they had come to sign the canal treaty, but they had informed Philippe that they would aid in the negotiation process. "All provisions of the treaty should first be discussed with Amador and Boyd, and you will proceed in strict accordance with them..."

But Philippe wouldn't be reduced to acting as a marionette to the Panamanians; he would sign the treaty himself.

When he arrived at John Hay's home, there were two reporters waiting at the entrance. "Are you going to sign the Canal Treaty, Mr. Minister?" they asked, almost simultaneously.

"Gentlemen, you seem to be better informed than I am!" Philippe said, smiling as he passed through the gate.

The Secretary of State received the Minister with absolute formality, "I have requested this meeting, Your Excellence, to sign, if you are in agreement, the treaty which will allow construction of the interoceanic canal. If Your Excellence accepts, we will proceed to read the document to be signed."

Philippe was in a hurry, "If Your Excellence agrees, we can do an abbreviated reading of the contract."

Once this formality had been finished, the Secretary of State asked Philippe, "Did you bring your seal to place on the document?"

Philippe apologized, "I've been taken by surprise, I didn't expect to sign right now and I didn't bring my seal..."

"If Your Excellence agrees, I could let you use the seal with my family's coat of arms so that we could consummate the treaty," Hay said. And so, the treaty was signed and formalized with the personal and familial seals of John Hay.

A few minutes later, Philippe left the residence holding the pen that the Secretary of State had given him as a memento of this important event. The canal would be constructed; Ferdinand de Lesseps' Grand Idea would live on forever and France's honor had been salvaged.

Philippe went directly to the telegram office and sent a cable to Francisco de La Espriella informing him that the treaty had been signed, and congratulating "the people for the successful completion of this trying but spectacular achievement." Then he went to the train station to wait for the Panamanian delegation to arrive.

Seeing them step down from the train and approach him, Philippe exclaimed enthusiastically, "From this day forward, the Republic of Panama is under the protection of the United States. The treaty has been signed!"

The elderly Dr. Amador nearly fainted. Federico Boyd held him up by the arm and demanded, "What are you saying? We specifically told you not to move forward with the treaty without consulting us!"

Carlos Arosemena exclaimed, "We clearly told you to wait for us! This can't be!"

The small Frenchman pretended to be concerned about the reactions of the newcomers. "I'm sorry gentlemen, the treaty has been signed. You are the ones who named me Minister Plenipotentiary. I only carried out my duty."

Federico Boyd approached Philippe and looking down on him, screamed, "Tomorrow morning we are going to Secretary Hay to demand negotiation of a new treaty!"

"Don't get your hopes up, Mr. Boyd. The negotiations are over. Now it is up to the United States Senate and the Panamanian Government to accept or reject the treaty, which incidentally will protect you against Colombia. Without a doubt, our friends to the south will leap at any opportunity to take Panama back…"

Overcome with rage, Boyd threw a punch at Philippe that sent him straight to the floor.

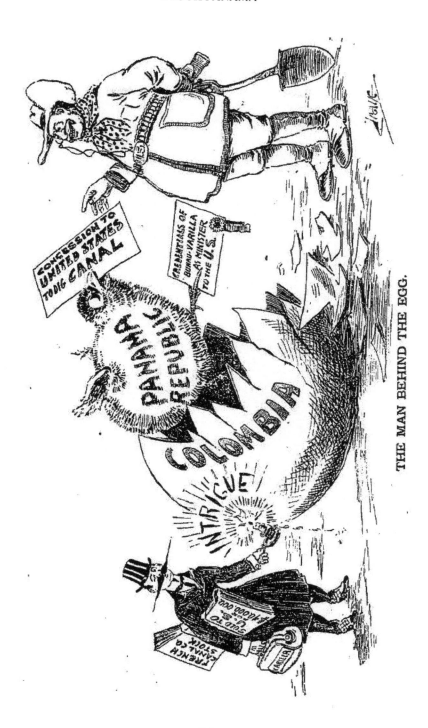

THE MAN BEHIND THE EGG.

Theodore Roosevelt Collection, Harvard College Library

Previous page: "The Man Behind the Egg," caricature by Craig published in 1903. Courtesy of The New York Times.

This page: President Roosevelt and President Amador at the entrance of the Panama City Cathedral years later. Theodore Roosevelt Collection, Harvard College Library. 560.52 1906-031.

38

Panama Canal Inauguration, August 1914

Nearly ten years had passed. When he was sure that the canal would be constructed and that Ferdinand de Lesseps' Grand Idea would be realized, Philippe stepped down from his position as Minister Plenipotentiary of the Republic of Panama. Since he knew that his beloved enterprise would be carried out, he asked the Panamanians to use the salaries owed to him to build a monument to his idol.

At fifty-five years old, Philippe was one of the few foreigners who made the journey to see the completion of the project that had cost so much in lives, time, and money, for the inauguration of the canal. He hadn't been invited but nevertheless, he had to be there.

Panama had changed a lot since the Americans had taken possession of the excavation. Thanks to the work of Dr. Gorgas, the same one Philippe had visited all those years ago in Cuba, tropical diseases had been controlled to the point that only fourteen workers had died of yellow fever that year.

Discipline and order prevailed on the isthmus, thanks to the work of John Stevens and later, Colonel George Washington Goethals, allowing the construction to advance as Philippe had dreamed during the time that he lived there. The railway had been relocated, a dam had been built, and the problem of the Chagres River had been resolved. The only vestige of problems from the past was the Culebra Cut, which continued to collapse, although with less frequency.

Crossing the canal aboard the steamer *Cristóbal*, which was surrounded by a large number of small sailboats and canoes heading to the Pacific as part of the celebration, Philippe hugged his daughter Giselle, who had accompanied him to the isthmus. He was moved by

the sensation of navigating between the formidable Culebra Cut.
He would never again return to Panama.

The Ancón crossing the recently inaugurated Panama Canal.
Photo courtesy of the Authority of the Panama Canal.

39

Tuesday, January 23, 1940, Paris, France.

Just before leaving for lunch, Eric Sevareid received a cable from his boss in New York, Edward R. Murrow, requesting him for a "special job." He was to look for Colonel Philippe-Jean Bunau-Varilla and, if he was still alive, interview the man about his participation in the construction of the Panama Canal.

Eric had worked for Columbia Broadcasting System for only five months and this was the first time his boss had asked him to do an interview, so this first assignment was quite exciting to him. Before leaving the office to meet his wife in a nearby bistro, he told his secretary to find out the whereabouts of the Colonel.

To his surprise, upon his return he found with the address and telephone number of Colonel Bunau-Varilla on his desk. The apartment seemed to be located in an exclusive area near the *Arc de Triomphe*. Without thinking too much about it, he immediately called and someone, a servant Eric assumed, answered the phone. In rather rudimentary French, having only studied at the *Alliance Française* for the past three months, he asked to speak to the Colonel on behalf of the Columbia Broadcasting System.

Soon after, a hoarse voice responded deliberately, and after involuntarily coughing into the phone, offered his cordial greeting in perfect English: "Good evening Mr. Sevareid, this is the Lieutenant Colonel Philippe-Jean Bunau-Varilla. How can I help you?"

When Sevareid explained the reason for his call, the voice became effusive, as if he had been waiting for a long time for someone to take an interest in his story. "Of course it would be a pleasure to be of service to the Columbia Broadcasting System, however I can. I think I have information of interest to the American people. What do you think about meeting with me at my home this afternoon?"

At four o'clock sharp, Eric arrived at the address the Colonel had given him. After being let inside by a butler, he was made to wait in an exquisitely decorated entrance that was undeniably larger than the apartment where the Sevareids lived. The temperature and the lighting were warm, somewhat comforting after the twenty minute walk through the frigid streets of Paris. "It pays to be in the French military!" he thought, smiling.

Eric listened as someone was approaching, limping down a corridor. Soon, Philippe appeared in the doorway. At eighty years old and with an enviable posture, the elderly soldier walked toward his guest with confidence in spite of his wooden prosthesis.

Extending his hand, the Colonel courteously greeted Eric, "Mr. Sevareid, welcome to my humble home. It's a pleasure to meet you!" And before Eric could respond, he continued, "Please, let's go to the library where we can visit freely."

Eric Sevareid had been in several opulent homes, but he had never seen one like that of the Bunau-Varilla family. When they entered the library, he was pleased to find two lavish armchairs near a lit fireplace carved out in stone. He took a seat and after a few minutes of conversation about Sevareid and his wife relocating to Paris, and the recent birth of their twins, the Colonel got right to the point:

"Mr. Sevareid, talk to me about this interview. I'm assuming you want to know all the details about every aspect of the construction of the Canal. I am absolutely at your service and want to assure you that I have an excellent memory. I don't forget anything! Furthermore, I have written several books and articles on the subject. I have several copies right here for you" he said with a broad smile, and then continued:

"Count on my full support so that the great American people will know the true history of the marvelous canal that our sister nations managed to complete, in spite of plans by the Germans!" Philippe exclaimed, emphasizing obvious disgust on the final word, as he motioned with his cane to make his point.

Eric settled into his seat, "Colonel, thank you for having me in your home. I think it would be a privilege for those who listen to the radio in the United States of America to hear your experiences in Panama. With respect to the program…"

Philippe was excited, "Yes, of course. All the time you need. We could estimate how many sessions we'd need to properly tell the story. You need only to tell me how many days you need me at the Columbia Broadcast System studios for the programs and I will happily assist you in this project, Mr. Sevareid. Also, if you need me to travel to New York for the interview, I will."

"Well, Colonel, it is actually only one program. We have five minutes. Have you heard of Robert Ripley's program, 'Believe it or Not!'?"

"Excuse me?" The intense blue eyes were indignant.

"Robert Ripley's program is dedicating a five minute spot to your story… It's a very popular program in the United States…" Eric said, visibly nervous.

Philippe sat in silence until he couldn't contain the explosion, "Impossible! This is a joke! The great history of the Panama Canal cannot be told in five minutes, Mr. Sevareid. The public deserves to hear the details as they happened, from the important people who were involved in the creation of the canal. It's too much information; to do it justice in five minutes is impossible! Thank you very much but I simply cannot accept such treatment given to my story. I'm sorry but I think it's best if you leave now."

Without knowing how to proceed, Eric got up and left his card on the table between the two chairs. "I'm very sorry to hear this, Colonel. I think there's been a misunderstanding and I'm sorry if I wasn't clear with you when I initially contacted you. If you change your mind, please call me. It would be lovely to include you in the program. Millions of people listen each week… Goodbye."

Mrs. Eric Sevareid and their twins, who in real life were born after the Bunau-Varilla interview. Photo: Library of Congress

40

The next day, Philippe contacted the young journalist and asked him to return. After all, the United States deserved to hear his story, even if it would be abbreviated.

During the following weeks, Philippe shared stories, photographs, and all his mementos with the young American. Since the elder Colonel was obviously very sick with something bronchial, Sevareid tried to make the sessions as short as possible so Philippe wouldn't get so tired.

The majority of their conversations revolved around Panama, but they also spoke about how Philippe enlisted in the war the same year that the canal was inaugurated and about how he had lost a leg during a bombing in Verdun.

It pleased Philippe to talk about his inventions, "During the war, I invented 'Verdunization,' which consisted of making the water potable by adding a small dose of chlorine. Today, this is done all over the world. And this leg," he said, smiling as he tapped it with his cane, "I invented that too!"

Sevareid had never known a person like Bunau-Varilla. It was incredible to think the man had done so much and Sevareid had never heard of him.

Finally, the date of the interview was determined to be February 17. "Colonel, we have to broadcast at four in the morning so the interview will be heard live during the program's normal hours in the United States. Since I live very close to the studio, I'd like to invite you to my house so we could wait together for the time of the broadcast. You can come to my apartment around midnight, we will have some tea with my wife, and later we'll go to the studio."

What Eric really wanted was to avoid having the old man walk to the studio in the middle of the night and expose his fragile lungs to the intense cold of those early morning hours.

When he arrived at the Sevareids' apartment, which was on the second floor, Philippe bowed slightly before handing a lovely box of chocolates to Lois, Eric's wife. Over the next few hours, they talked peacefully over tea in the living room. Every once in a while, Lois would go to check on the baby twins who were sleeping in the adjacent bedroom.

Making the most of the last few minutes before leaving the study, Eric wanted to ask a few more questions. Not because they would be used for the program, but because after speaking at length with Philippe and thorough consideration of the French failure to complete the Panama Canal, he was curious:

"Colonel, Bunau-Varilla, are you and your brother still partners?"

Surprised by the question, Philippe simply responded, "My brother is my brother; he is a good man but we have our differences. I'm not going to speak about him."

"May I ask you another question?"

Philippe stared at the young reporter. There was something he didn't like about the younger man's tone, but he nodded and sipped his tea.

"Is it true that when William Nelson Cromwell came to Paris, just before the secession of Panama, he and your brother bought a massive quantity of Canal Company shares for a group of renowned Republican politicians?" Sevareid asked, cautiously.

Philippe whacked his cane on the table in front of him, shattering a vase, "It's not true! What I did, I did for France, for our honor!" he shouted before having to stop due to a violent coughing fit. Eric thought that the elderly colonel would die right there. When he could breathe, Philippe finished, "It's always the same thing!"

The noise woke the babies and Lois came to see what was taking place, "Eric, what's happening? Are you okay?"

"It's nothing, my love, go and check on the babies..." a distressed Sevareid responded.

Once Philippe had calmed down, he accepted a glass of water from Lois. "My apologies, madam."

"No, I'm sorry if I have offended you, Colonel. I only wanted to know..." Eric Sevareid said while motioning for his wife to return to the babies.

"I think it's time for us to go, Mr. Sevareid. We only have twenty minutes until the broadcast. Please give my thanks to your wife. Tell her I'm very sorry for having awakened the babies."

"Colonel, one more thing…" Eric didn't know how to say it, but he had to do it before they left. "Today I was advised from New York that the broadcast will only last three minutes. Problems with programming, I'm very sorry…"

Philippe sighed. For a few seconds he looked through the window at the snow falling outside, and then smiled at the young reporter, "Well, Mr. Sevareid, then it's best that we make the most of our time!"

Minutes later, from the window, Lois Sevareid watched as the men crossed the street. Her husband walked one step behind the diminutive elder Colonel Bunau-Varilla, who in spite of his wooden leg, walked erect, with his head held high, to tell the truth about the history of the Panama Canal.

THE END

Philippe Bunau-Varilla as an older man.
Notice the cane he used to walk after having lost a leg in the Battle of
Verdun during the First World War. Photograph: Corbis Images

EPILOGUE

Philippe Bunau-Varilla died on the 18th of May, 1940, at an American hospital in Paris, shortly after his interview with Eric Sevareid and just as the Germans began invading France during the Second World War. The funeral was attended by a small group of government officials and his family, with the exception of his daughter Giselle, who was in Kenya with her husband, and Etienne, who was serving in the French Air Force.

Etienne, who had received a *Voisin* plane as a graduation gift from his father, had become one of the first French pilots. During the First World War, a bomber he piloted was shot down in Speyer, but Etienne survived only to be captured and held hostage until his release during a prisoner exchange.

Maurice Bunau-Varilla, who sided with the Germans because of their anti-Marxist views, allowed the invading forces to use his newspaper, *Le Matin*, as an official publication during the occupation. Maurice died before the war ended and his son Jean-Guy, who worked at *Le Matin*, was accused of collaborating with the enemy. As a consequence, the family fortune was confiscated and Maurice was sentenced to life in prison. Although he was released in 1953, he is said to have committed suicide soon after.

Without the involvement of Philippe Bunau-Varilla, the Panama Canal, and perhaps the Republic of Panama, probably would not exist as we know them today.

If you enjoyed the book, please "Like" it on Facebook!

www.facebook.com/itookpanama

References

In addition to the people mentioned in the Acknowledgments section of the book, the writer used the following works as reference during the research process:

Bunau-Varilla, Philippe. The Great Adventure of Panama. Dodo Press, 2010

Bunau-Varilla, Philippe, Panama, the creation, destruction, and resurrection. McBride, Nast & Company, 1914

Bunau-Varilla, Philippe, From Panama to Verdun. Philadelphia Dorrance and Company, 1940

Anguizola, Gustave, Philippe Bunau-Varilla, The Man Behind the Panama Canal. Nelson Hall, 1980

McCullough, David. The Path Between the Seas, Simon & Schuster, 1977

Morris, Edmund. Theodore Rex, Random House, 2001

Loizillon, Gabriel. The Bunau-Varilla Brothers and the Panama Canal. Lulu, 2008

Sevareid, Eric. The Man Who Invented Panama, American Heritage Magazine, Volume 14, Issue 5, 1963

71889897R00082

Made in the USA
Middletown, DE
30 April 2018